Harmony

Harmony

BY

TRACY WILSON

http://beautifulpublications.com

Published by
Beautiful Publications LLC
Stratford, CT 06614

This book is a work of fiction. Names, characters, places, and incidents are either products of the *author's* imagination or are used fictitiously. Any resemblance to actual events or locales or persons, living or dead, is entirely coincidental.

PRINT ISBN: 978-1-7362753-8-2
EBOOK ISBN: 978-1-7362753-9-9

Printed in the United States of America

Disclaimer

This is fiction. This is **<u>NOT</u>** a true story. My mother-in-law was kind, compassionate, and soft-spoken. I never had any problems with her. The woman I'm writing about is someone else's nightmare – not mine.

Chapter 23

"Excuse me – Ms. Wilkins..." Charles said as he tried to get Helen's attention...

"I'm in a hurry..." she barked...

"Yes Maam – I can see that – Mr. Wilkins wanted me to give you these..." he said as he took the keys out his pocket and gave them to her...

"Thanks – but I already have keys..."

"Ms. Wilkins – those are the keys to your place..."

"My place?"

"Yes Maam – you live in Unit 2J – right?"

"Hell no I don't live up there!"

"Ms. Wilkins – I'm sorry – I helped Mr. Wilkins move all of your things upstairs while you were gone yesterday..."

"What?!"

"Yes Maam – all your things are in your place... and I was told to give you the keys as soon as I saw you..."

"We'll see about this!" she snapped as she got on the elevator... "Mutha fucka think he can just put me out like this – fuck him..." she said as she went inside... "Well, well... what do we have here?" she asked as she looked on the sectional and saw the gift box I have him... "Harland – you probably don't even realize you lost your key to her house... Hmmm... I'll get this right back to you – I just need to make a copy for myself first..." she said as she put the box in her pocket and went out the door...

"Mmm... good morning..." Harland breathed...

"Good morning..." I yawned...

"What would you like to do today?"

"You..." I breathed as I pulled him into a kiss..."

"Sounds good... but we need to eat..." he said as he got up...

"Okay..." I sighed as I got up, put on my robe, and went into the living room...

"Sorry we have to have breakfast on the couch..." he said as he started making coffee...

"That's okay – I do that all the time..."

"I wanna go buy another table today – and I'd like to buy something else..."

"Oh boy – what else?" I laughed...

"I'd like to buy another desk... another chair... another computer..."

"Harland..."

"I know – you're not moving in... yet..."

"How may I help you?" the associate asked...

"I'd like to make a copy of this key..." Helen answered as she handed him the box...

"Hmmm – we have that key in stock – but the only colors we have are silver and gold..."

"I'll take it in silver..."

"Okay – would you like a gift box for the silver key as well?"

"No thank you..."

"I'll be right back..." Helen looked around as if she was expecting someone to walk in and catch her doing something she had no business doing... "Is everything alright?"

"Everything's fine – why?"

"You seem nervous..." he answered as he rang up her purchase...

"Thank you..."

"You're welcome – have a good day..." he said to the breeze she left behind her as she slammed the door...

"Coffee?" Harland asked, knowing damn well I wanted some...

"Yes – thank you!" I exclaimed as I took the cup and began sipping it...

"What can I make you for breakfast?"

"Surprise me..."

"Okay..." I watched intently as he took out the apple-muffin mix...

"Ooohhh..." Harland smiled as he took eggs, Swiss cheese, crumbled sausage, chopped onions, chopped peppers, and half & half creamer out the refrigerator and put them on the counter as we heard knocking...

"Who is it?" I asked...

"It's Helen..." I looked at Harland before I opened the door...

"Good morning..."

"Good morning Harmony, good morning Harland..."

"Good morning Ma..."

"I just came by to bring you this..." she said as she placed the gift box on the counter...

"Thanks – it must've fallen out my pocket..." he said as he picked it up, opened it to make sure the key was inside, and put it in his robe pocket...

"What happened to the table?"

"I broke it..."

"How the hell did you do that?" she laughed...

"I'm getting another one..." he answered, ignoring her question...

"Smells good..."

"I have coffee – you want some?"

"I don't wanna intrude..."

"Ma – stop it..."

"Okay – yes – I'd like some coffee..." she said as she came to sit down beside me...

"Here..."

"Thank you..." she said as she took the cup and took a sip...

"Harmony – I want to apologize for the way I spoke to you yesterday..."

"Thank you..." I acknowledged...

"A lot's happened in a short amount of time – I know that's no excuse – but that's all I got..." she laughed nervously...

"I accept your apology..." I said as we hugged. Harland smiled as he began making plates...

"Have you had anything to eat Ma?"

"No – I haven't had a chance to go shopping..."

"We're going shopping later today – I could drop you off at Stop & Shop if you want..."

"I don't want to intrude..."

"Ma – what'd I tell you about that?"

"Okay, okay..." she laughed as he handed us plates... "Ohh... this looks good..." Helen said...

"Oh my God – it's delicious!" I exclaimed...

"You're in for a treat – my son is an excellent cook..." she said as we continued eating...

"Ma – now that your things are upstairs, do you like it?"

"I like it..." she lied...

"Good..."

"It's quiet... it's comfortable..."

"I'm glad..."

"Well – I'm going to head upstairs – call me when you're ready to go and I'll meet you out in the lobby..." she said as she got up...

"Alright Ma – we'll see you later..." Harland said as she left... "Come here..." he commanded as he pulled me into his arms and kissed me...

"Wow – what did I do to deserve that?"

"I never thought I'd see you hug my mother..."

"I know – right?" I laughed...

"Gotcha!" Helen exclaimed as she went into her condo and slammed her door...

"Thanks for taking me to Stop & Shop..." Helen said as she got in the front seat...

"You're welcome..." Harland said as he got in and I got in the back...

"What else are you buying besides another table?"

"Whatever Harmony wants for the office..."

"Office?"

"Yea – since I gave you the bed that was in the guest room – we're turning the guest room into an office..."

"Don't you have your father's desk in there already?"

"Yes Ma..." he sighed. I was glad we were pulling up to Stop & Shop...

"Have a nice day Helen..." I said as I got out the car...

"I thought you were going with Harland?"

"I am..." I said as I opened the front door and got in...

"I'll call you when I'm ready for you to pick me up..." she said...

"Bye Ma..." he said as we pulled out the parking lot...

"Harland – I know you want me to move in – but..."

"Harmony – let's not talk about that right now – okay?" he asked as he squeezed my hand...

"Okay..." I sighed. I looked out the window as we headed back towards Bob's Discount Furniture. They have a show room where you can walk around and look as much as you like – plus, they have a candy and ice cream room with tables and I was looking forward to getting some caramel chews...

"We're here..." he said as he parked the car. I didn't wait for him to open the door for me – I got out and waited...

"I'm glad you're excited..."

"I am!" I exclaimed as we went towards the entrance...

"Mutha fucka gonna just drop me off like I'm a passenger in a taxi – before that Bitch came along he would park the car, go inside with me, and pay for the fuckin' groceries!" Helen snapped as she snatched a cart and went inside...

"Mr. Wilkins – how are you?" the manager greeted...

"I'm good..."

"How can we help you today?"

"We're here to look at office furniture..." he answered as he pulled me close to him and wrapped his arm around me...

"We have a few new pieces... and we have some pieces in the pit – follow me..." the manager said as he turned to walk and we followed him...

"Now I gotta ask somebody to help me with this..." Helen exclaimed...

"Ms. Wilkins – let me help you with that..." Charles said as he took the jars down off the shelf...

"Thank you Charles..."

"You're welcome..."

"I'm done with my shopping – I can keep you company if you like..."

"I'd like that Charles..." she answered as she smiled... "I'm sorry about earlier today..."

"Don't worry about it Ms. Wilkins..."

"Please – call me Helen..."

"My mother's name was Helen..." Charles sighed as they continued to walk up and down the aisles...

"I want this desk!" I exclaimed...

"I don't believe it!" the manager exclaimed...

"What's wrong?" Harland asked...

"We've been trying to get rid of that desk for a few weeks!"

"I'm glad I got it – put sold on it before anybody else gets it!" I squealed...

"Yes Maam!" the manager laughed...

"Don't forget the chair..." Harland reminded him...

"I'll put a sold sign on both..." the manager laughed again...

"How are you getting home from here?" Charles asked...

"I told my son I'd let him know when I was ready..."

"I can take you home..."

"Charles – that's sweet of you – thank you!"

"You're welcome... Helen..." he said as he smiled...

"I love this..." I sighed as we went to sit at the table...

"Me too..." Harland agreed...

"They always have my favorite candy..."

"And Hagen Daaz..."

"Thank you for the secretary's desk..."

"Is that what that is?"

"Yea..."

"Why do they call it that?"

"According to Greg Jaron of Jaron's furniture, that piece was actually used by the Secretary of an Estate as a place to pay the bills and handle the affairs of a large household. According to the design Toscano blog, the term comes from the French word secretaire, which is a term for a rectangle desk that's taller than it is wider..."

"How'd you know that?"

"I googled it..." I laughed...

"I wonder if the Secretary of the State has a Secretary's Desk..."

"Probably..."

"Well I'm glad you're happy..."

"I am Harland..."

"What else can I get you?"

"Well... since you're asking... when I was in high school I found an old typewriter with the red and black ribbon..."

"I'll look on amazon – they might not have the one you found in high school, but I'm sure they have something close to it..."

"Thank you..."

"I'm going to get you an HP All-In-One computer and printer too..."

"How'd you know that's what I have at home?"

"I looked in your office..."

"Mr. Wilkins – you're all set – we can have that delivered to you tomorrow..." the manager said as he came over to us...

"You deliver on Sundays?" Harland asked...

"We do local deliveries – you practically live around the corner from us – so..."

"Thanks – I appreciate it..." Harland said as he signed the receipt...

"We appreciate you too..." the manager said as he took the original receipt and gave Harland a copy...

"You ready to go home?"

"Yea..." I sighed...

"Thank you again Charles – I really appreciate it..." Helen said as she opened her door...

"Let me get the bags for you..." Charles said as he brought the bags inside... "Your furniture looks good in here..."

"Thanks – I like it too..."

"I'm glad – you were so mad earlier..."

"I know – I'm sorry about that – I lived in my house for so long – I haven't lived anywhere else – my husband bought us the house when we first got married..." she sighed as she started to tear up...

"Helen... you're upset..." Charles said as he pulled her into a hug and held her...

"I'm sorry..."

"You don't need to apologize..."

"It's been so long..."

"How long since your husband passed away?"

"My husband isn't dead..."

"You're still married?!"

"The day my husband left me is the day I got divorced..." she sighed...

"Helen... I'm so sorry..."

"If my son didn't step up and take care of me... I don't know where I'd be..." she said as she started crying...

"Helen... No..." he breathed as he kissed her. Helen wrapped her arms around him as they tongued each other down...

"Hmmm – my mother hasn't called or texted..." Harland said as he opened the door and we went inside...

"Maybe she took an uber home..."

"Naa – she would've called me or text me – le'me check the GPS..." he said as he went to turn on his laptop... "Hmmm – that's strange – it's showing that she's here – but she's not here..."

"Why don't we go check on her?"

"You don't mind?"

"Once we know she's alright we can come back downstairs..." I said as I opened the door and we went to get in the elevator...

"Oh Charles... Yes... Don't stop..."

"Helen... Helen... Helen..."

"You know – I just realized – Charles wasn't in the lobby when we came in..." Harland said...

"Maybe he has the day off..." When we got off the elevator, we put our hands over our mouths to keep from laughing out loud...

"Charles... Oh yes..."

"Helen... You feel so good... Oh shit..."

"It's been so long... I need this dick... give it to me... I'm 'bout to cum..."

"Oh Helen... I'm cummin' with you..."

"Charles! Charles! Charles! Aaahh!!"

"Ohh... Ohh.. Ohh... Ohh... Oohhhhhh!!"

"Can I see you again?" she breathed...

"You can see me anytime you want..."

"Come back later tonight – I'll make dinner..."

"I'll definitely be back for dinner... and dessert..." he said as he back out the door right into Harland...

"Hello Charles..."

"Oh my God – Mr. Wilkins – it's not what you think – I..."

"Charles – it's fine..."

"You not mad?"

"No Charles – I'm not mad..."

"Charles – who are you talking to?" Helen asked as she opened the door... "What the hell you doin' here?" she snapped...

"You said you were going to call me when you were ready to be picked up..."

"Charles was at Stop & Shop – he offered me a ride home..."

"Thank you Charles..." Harland said...

"Well – I need to put these groceries away – I'll talk to y'all later..." she said as she went back in her place and closed the door...

"I guess she told us!" I laughed...

"She sure did!" Harland laughed. Charles didn't say anything. We all got the elevator without speaking. Charles got off on the 3rd floor...

"Good night..."

"Good night..." we both said. We took the elevator back downstairs, went back inside, and laughed our asses off...

"Aaaa Haaaa! Aaaa Haaaa! Aaaa Haaaa! Aaaa Haaaa! Aaaa Haaaa! Aaaa Haaaa! Aaaa Haaaa! Aaaa Haaaa! Aaaa Haaaa! Aaaa Haaaa! Aaaa Haaaa! Aaaa Haaaa!"

Chapter 25

"You want this dick?" Harland growled...

"Yes! Oh God! Harland! Fuck me! I'm cumming!"

"Uugh! Uugh! Uugh! Uugh! Uuuggghhh!!" Harland fell down on top of me and I bust out laughing... "Umm... what's so funny?"

'I can't help it...' I laughed...

"You can't help what?" he asked as he lay beside me and propped his head up on his arm...

"I keep thinking about your mother!" I laughed...

"I... I don't get it..."

"You asked me did I want your dick..." I laughed...

"You weren't laughing..."

"Your mother said... Your mother said..." I couldn't stop laughing...

"My mother said it's been so long since I've had dick – give it to me!" We were both laughing so hard we were crying and holding our stomachs...

"Oh my God – you sounded just like her – I can't!"

"I used to hear my parents having sex when I was young – but most of the time I heard moaning and music..."

"I heard the same thing – along with the bed bangin'..." I laughed...

"Yea – that too!" Harland laughed...

"Do you think Charles can hear us?"

"Naa – our bedroom faces the side of the building – he'd have to leave the lobby and stand by the door to hear us..."

"You think he's ever done that?"

"You're the loudest one I've had in here..."

"That many?" I asked as I sat up..."

"Harmony..." he breathed as he pulled me into a kiss... "You're the first woman I've had here in a long time..."

"I'm sorry – when you said that..."

"No – I'm sorry – I didn't mean it like that..."

"So... Charles... and your mother..."

"Yea..."

"You're really okay with it?"

"I'm okay with it..."

"Maybe your mother will... never mind..."

"Maybe my mother will be a better person?"

"Yea..."

"I hope so..."

"Mutha fucka came up here yesterday checkin' on me like I'm his got-damned child – you wasn't thinkin' 'bout me when you took that Bitch shoppin' – what if Charles wasn't there – I guess I was supposed to find my own way home – meanwhile that Bitch jumps in the front seat as soon as I get out the car – that's okay though – I got somethin' for that ass..."

"Hello Sheddi..." Harland answered...

"Harland – I have news..."

"Okay..."

"We can close tomorrow!"

"That's great!"

"I contacted your attorney and the other realtor contacted the seller's attorney – we're all set for tomorrow at 10 a.m...."

"Okay – I'll see you tomorrow morning..." he said and then he hung up...

"Good news?" I asked...

"The best!"

"Tell me!"

"We close tomorrow!"

"Harland – that's great!" I exclaimed as we kissed...

"It sure is – once I get the check I can pay off my mother's mortgage and mine..."

"I wish I could pay off my mortgage..." I sighed...

"You could always sell your house..." he breathed as he kissed me... "And move in with me..."

"You're right..." I could..." I acknowledged as we heard knocking...

"Who is it?" Harland yelled...

"Bobs!"

"Hold on..." he said as he jumped up, put on his pants and his robe, and ran to open the door...

"Did you forget we were coming?" the delivery guy asked as I put on my robe, tied it around me, put on my slippers, and went out into the living room...

"Yea..."

"Where would you like this?" the delivery guy asked...

"Right in here..." Harland answered as he showed them to the office...

"Okay – I'll be right back..." he said as he started to leave...

"You don't have anybody to help you?"

"I don't need anybody to help me..." he answered as he went to get the desk...

"Well excuse me..." Harland laughed. The delivery guy came back with the chair first...

"This is the heaviest piece..." he laughed...

"Oh okay – you got jokes..." Harland laughed as the delivery guy went to get the actual desk. When he came back inside, he had the desk on a dolly... "Oh okay playa... I see how you do..." The delivery guy just smiled as he took the desk into the office. Harland continued to stand, I continued to sit, and the delivery guy went back and forth until he brought in the final piece... "Thank you – but I didn't realize we had to put it together..." Harland said...

"I gotchu..." the delivery man said as he went back outside. When he came back inside, he had a tool box with him. Harland watched him go into the office, sit down in the chair, open the tool box, and put the desk together in a few minutes...

"You're all set..." the delivery man said as he came out the office...

"What's your name?"

"Rob..."

"Thanks Rob – I appreciate you..." Harland said as he handed him $100 dollar bill..."

"You're welcome – have a good day – call if you have any problems..." he said as he left...

"Come see your new desk..." I got up and went into the office...

"Oh Harland!" I exclaimed...

"You like it?"

"I love it! Thank you!"

"You're welcome..." he breathed as he pulled me into a kiss. Harland held me for a few minutes and then we went back into the living room... "Are you staying here tonight?"

"I'm not sure..."

"You can stay here..."

"You have to be ready for the closing tomorrow..."

"You can take the day off – you can come with me – we can celebrate..."

"Oh no – I'm going to work – you don't need me there – your mother will probably want to go..."

"I'm not telling my mother..."

"You're not?"

"No..."

"Why not?"

"I think it's better if I let my mother think I'm not closing until next week..."

"I'm surprised – I figured you'd want your mother there with you..."

"I did – but the way she's been acting lately – I don't want her to be anywhere near the closing – I don't even want her to meet Sheddi after the way she spoke to her..."

"Now I really don't think I should be there..." I sighed...

"Why not?"

"If your mother finds out I had anything to do with your closing, we'll both catch hell – instead of hugging her, I might end up chocking her!" I laughed...

"Okay – I get it – I'll go to the closing by myself!" he laughed...

"I'd love to celebrate with you, but I don't know how your mother will react..."

"I don't care how my mother's going to react – after the closing we're going to celebrate – and you're going to be there whether she likes it or not!"

"Yes Daddy..." I said as I went over to him and put my arms around his neck...

"That's more like it..." he breathed as he pulled me close to him and kissed me hard as he squeezed my ass... "You're spending the night with me..." he breathed as he kissed me again... "And I'm not taking no for an answer..." he breathed as he kissed me again and pushed his tongue in my mouth...

"Okay..." I relented as I pushed him away from me... "I'll stay tonight – but I'm going home tomorrow..."

"No..." he said as he pulled me back into his arms... "You're not..."

"Harland – I don't have enough clothes here..."

"I'll take you shopping..."

"Harland – I'll stay tonight – but I'm going home tomorrow..."

"I'm picking you up from the train..."

"Okay..."

"I'm taking you out to celebrate..."

"Okay..."

"And then I'm going to kidnap you..." he laughed...

"How 'bout this..." I started to say as he interrupted me by kissing me... "I'll stay tonight..."

"Sounds good..." he breathed as he kissed me again...

"I go to work tomorrow..."

"Okay..." he breathed as he kissed me again...

"You pick me up from the train..."

"Go on..." he breathed as he kissed me again...

"You take me out to dinner..."

"Go on..." he breathed as he kissed me again...

"And we go back to my house for dessert?"

"I won't leave..." he breathed as he kissed me again...

"I don't want you to leave..." I breathed as I kissed him back. We continued kissing as he pushed me back towards the couch. We sat down on the couch and he started to push me down on my back but I stopped him... "Harland – wait..."

"Wait? Why?"

"I'm feeling a lil' light headed..."

"Okay – I'll make us some coffee – but you owe me – and when I come to collect, I expect payment in full..."

"I'm going to need more than coffee..." I laughed...

"It's open..." Helen said as she heard knocking...

"Good morning..." Charles said as he came inside and closed the door...

"Good morning..." Helen said as she walked over to him, put her arms around him, and kissed him fully...

"Oh my – I could get used to this..." he breathed as he kissed her back...

"I made coffee..."

"Smells good..." he said as she handed him a cup, picked up a cup for herself, and they both took a sip...

"Can I ask you a question?"

"Sure..." Harland answered as he handed me a cup of coffee and sat down beside me...

"Are you going to have to go to another closing to pay off the mortgages?"

"No..." he answered as he took a sip of his coffee... "Everything will be done tomorrow..."

"That's a lot..."

"Actually – it's not..."

"It's not?"

"I offered full asking on my mother's place upstairs – normally I'd have to put down 20 percent but since I'm paying 100 percent, it cuts down on the closing costs – I already own this place so all I had to do was get a statement from the lender with a pay-off amount..."

"It still seems like a lot..."

"It's not – the hardest thing I'll have to deal with tomorrow is paperwork – I'll have to sign at least 40 pages!" he laughed...

"Oh God – I remember that – my hand and wrist started to cramp up on me!" I laughed...

"I might have to soak my wrist afterwards..." he laughed...

"Are you going to have any money left after this is all said and done?"

'I'm not broke!" he laughed...

"That's not what I mean..."

"What do you mean?"

"You're selling your house – you're using that money to pay off your place and your mother's place – you have to pay your attorney – you have to pay your realtor – after everybody gets paid..."

"Harmony – I'm going to be better off than I am now..."

"How?"

"I'm paying my mortgage every month. Before the house was paid off, I paid that mortgage off. Once the mortgage was paid off, I continued to pay the other bills and the taxes. I went from paying $3,600 a month to $3,600 a month..."

"That doesn't make any sense..." I laughed...

"The mortgage is paid off on the house – but I paid the taxes plus the other bills – it was if I was still paying two mortgages..."

"Wow – you paid for two properties here in Connecticut – in New York you'd pay $3,600 for one property – and that doesn't include utilities..."

"I know – that's why I can't wait until after the closing – I'm going from paying $3,600 a month to $1,345 a month – and that includes my mother's maintenance and taxes..."

"Oh my God!"

"I'm putting over $2,000 a month back in my pocket – that's equivalent to my job giving me a hefty raise – even if I get promoted it won't give me an extra $2,000 a month..."

"I'm so happy for you..."

"I'm happy for me too – and the best part is I'll still be able to take care of my mother..."

"Are you putting anything in her name?"

"Absolutely not – I'm leaving everything the way it is – she can continue to do whatever she wants – I'm saving money · I won't have to worry about raking leaves, shoveling snow, cutting grass – Harmony – who does all that for you?"

"I have a guy – Alex comes over with two other guys – they clean the gutters, they rake the leaves, they cut the grass, and they shovel the snow..."

"You'd save a lot of money if you'd sell your house and move in with me..."

"Harland – if I move in with you – we need a bigger place..."

"Wait a minute – you want kids?" he laughed...

"Hell no!" I laughed... "Oh wait – that didn't come out right..."

"Yes it did – I don't want kids either..." he laughed...

"I have 3 bedrooms – I have an office too – plus, your closet isn't big enough to hold all my clothes – and I have a garage full of keepsakes..."

"I love you..." he breathed as he kissed me...

"What was that for?"

"You just told me you're actually thinking about moving in with me..."

"Harland – I..." he cut me off by pushing his tongue in my mouth, pushing me back on the couch, and spreading my legs. Once he thrust himself inside me and I started moaning as I grabbed his ass and pushed him in deeper, he knew he'd won the battle...

Chapter 26

"I wish you didn't have to leave..." Helen sighed...

"I wish I didn't have to leave either..." Charles breathed as he pulled her into a kiss...

"Will you be back tonight?"

"Why don't you come by my place instead?"

"I'd like that..."

"I get off work tonight at 8 – I can come get you..." he breathed as he kissed her again... or you can meet me upstairs..."

"I don't know where you live..." Helen laughed...

"I live in apartment 3L"

"I want you to come get me..."

"I'll come get you..."

"I like waking up to morning dick..."

"And I like giving it to you..." he breathed as he kissed her again...

"You better get up and get in the shower..."

"You better get up and join me..."

"If I get in the shower with you – you ain't goin' to work..."

"Okay – but tonight, I'm not taking no for an answer..." he breathed as he kissed her again...

"Charles – get up..."

"Okay, okay..." he laughed as he got up out the bed..."

"Turn around baby..." Charles turned around so she could admire his naked body... "Damn you look good..."

"Thank you Baby..." he said as he went to get in the shower...

"I don't wanna go..." I groaned as Siri started singing her song...

"You don't have to go..." Harland breathed as he kissed me...

"I better get up..." I sighed and then I got up out the bed...

"Can I come?"

"C'mon on..." I sighed as I went into the bathroom. Harland beat me to the shower so I let him turn it on. I was so tempted to stay home with him instead of going to work, but I kept telling myself to go to work...

"You comin'?"

"Yea..." I sighed as I stepped into the shower. As soon as we got under the water, he pulled me into a kiss... "Harland – stop it..."

"Why?"

"I can't get my hair wet – I don't have time to dry it..."

"Oh... Sorry..." I could tell he was relieved that it was about my hair and not because I didn't want him. I took a really quick shower, got out, and started drying myself off... "So you just gonna leave me in here like this?" he asked as he turned sideways and I saw his dick was fully erect...

"Baby I'm sorry – I can't..."

"Fine..." he sighed as he started washing himself. I started to go into a trance watching the soap cascade down his body and I had to shake my head to snap myself out of it..."

"What's wrong?"

"Nothing – I'm going to get dressed..." I answered as I left the bathroom. When he came out the bathroom I was already dressed...

"Damn you got dressed quick!"

"I know..."

"You in a hurry?"

"Get dressed Harland..." I laughed. He sat down on the bed, turned his back to me, and got dressed. When he was done, he went in front of the mirror to adjust his shirt and I went up behind him...

"Uh uh – what are you doing?"

"I'm making sure you have a good day..." I answered as I turned him to face me, pulled him back towards the bed, sat down on the edge, and opened his pants...

"Harmony – I want to make sure you get to the train... Ooohhh...." he moaned as I took his dick in my mouth. I wanted to take my time – I wanted to caress it – I wanted to deep throat it – but we didn't have a lot of time – it was 5:45 a.m. – so I had to make it good – and make it quick..."

"Oh shit!" he exclaimed as he grabbed my head on both sides and began fucking my mouth...

"Mmm... Mmm... Mmm..." I moaned on his dick as I sucked hungrily and sloppily. Spit was dripping out my mouth and onto his balls as he pushed his dick in further...

"Harmony... Fuck!" he moaned as I relaxed my jaws and felt his dick in the back of my throat... "Harmony... Fuck... I'm cumming... I'm cumming... Aaaahhhh!" I swallowed and continued sucking softly as he played in my hair... "Damn..." he breathed...

"You okay?" I asked as I looked up at him...

"I love you..."

"I love you too..."

"It's 6 o'clock..."

"I'm ready..." I said as I got up...

"Not so fast..." he breathed as he pulled me into a kiss and held me...

"I love you too..." I sighed. Harland let go of me, we got our phones, chargers, etc., and went out the door...

Chapter 27

"Hey Ladies!"

"Hey!" Yyanna said...

"Harmony – where are you?" Snow asked...

"I'm at lunch..."

"Oh okay – I'm not used to you calling us during the day...

"Oh my God – I have so much to tell y'all..." I said as I started eating..."

"What are you eating?" Yyanna asked...

"Tacos..."

"You so damn rude – how you gonna call us and eat tacos while you talkin' to us?" Snow laughed...

"Snow – I don't have a lot of time – Harland's coming over tonight so I won't be able to call y'all..."

"Alright – go 'head..."

"Well – I did what you said – and baby..."

"What happened?" they both asked...

"She started as soon as I got in the house..."

"You didn't leave?" Snow asked...

"Nope..."

"I thought we had an understanding!"

"Oh we had an understanding alright – I wanted to see my man – I wasn't going anywhere!"

"I know that's right!" Yyanna exclaimed...

"So I saw Harland made some changes since his mother moved in, I said it was nice, and I asked where the furniture was – she gonna say you didn't see that pods outside – I said to be honest I only saw you and Harland..."

"That's right Harmony!" Snow exclaimed...

"So I'm on my way to the bathroom and she says umm... where are you going?"

"No the fuck she didn't!" Yyanna said as she shook her head...

"I told her I was going to the bathroom and she says well – make sure you stay outta my room..."

"See – I can't – how the fuck she tryin' to tell you what the fuck to do in his house – Harmony you good – I don't give a fuck – I would 'a cursed Flick's mother out – I'm sorry..."

"I did..."

"What?!" they both exclaimed...

"I'm getting to that..." I said as I finished a taco... "I told her I've already seen your room, and I went to pee. When I came out the bathroom, Helen was sitting on the couch and Harland was at the table so I sat down with him and asked him how's everything going with the house – she says that's none of your business..."

"I swear to God Harmony – you better not be lyin' – you cursed her out – right?" Snow asked...

"I'm getting to that..." I said as I started eating another taco... "Harland told me they got everything out – it went smooth – thanks to his friends James and Alex..."

"Harmony – Harland didn't check his mother?" Yyanna asked...

"No..." I answered as Snow crossed her arms and got closer to the screen, waiting for me to tell her when I cursed his mother out... "So he said he was tired and I told him I'd give him a massage – this Bitch gonna ask me and just where do you think you're going to be massaging him at – so I said wherever he wants..."

"I know that's the fuck right – that's what I'm talkin' about!" Snow exclaimed...

"What did his mother say?" Yyanna asked...

"She ain't say shit!" I laughed...

"I know that's right – I wish the fuck Flick's mother would – I'd tell her I'ma start with his dick and move around to his balls!" she exclaimed as we all laughed...

"So he asked if I had dinner and I didn't so he ordered from Thelma's – I got shrimp – they got chicken – before he can place the order she tells me I need to order some vegetables..."

"What the fuck – is she skinny?" Yyanna asked...

"No..." I answered as I shook my head...

"Yo – this Bitch – I can't!" Snow exclaimed...

"So I wanted some chicken so she says if you wanted some chicken you should 'a ordered some chicken – Harland gives me some chicken so, to be petty, I offered his mother some shrimp..."

"Oh you good..." Snow said...

"She took some?" Yyanna asked...

"Sure did..." I answered... "So Harland asked how my day was and I say it was long – his mother asks where I work – I say Fair Hearings – she says you mean DSS · I said yea that's right – she gonna say you should 'a just said that – I told her I said what I wanted to say..."

"Oh shit... you was ready!" Yyanna said...

"Girl – Harland hurried up and interrupted that – talkin' 'bout ummm so how long are you staying?"

"See – why the fuck didn't he check his mother – Flick would 'a been checked his mother..."

"I swear I thought that man would never check his mother – but baby..."

"Oh shit – what time is lunch over?" Snow asked...

"1 o'clock..."

"You goin' back late – I gotta hear this!"

"Okay so I told you what happened when we got the food – this is what happened before we got the food – Harland went out into the hall and this Bitch gonna say Harmony – le'me tell you one mutha-fuckin' thing – I'm not going anywhere!"

"Harmony..." Snow started to say..."

"I said hmmm – you sure about that? Last I heard you were going to hell..."

"Yo! That's what the fuck I'm talkin' about!" Snow exclaimed as she high-fived herself...

"Damn Harmony – you told the Bitch she was goin' to hell!" Yyanna laughed...

"So I said I was going home 'cause I was tired but Harland said you're staying so she says I'm going to my room – thanks for dinner – he wants me to spend the night with him – I told him absolutely not – he gon' tell me my mother goes to sleep early!" I laughed...

"Oh hell no!" Snow exclaimed...

"Bitch might wake up in the middle of the night and attack your ass..." Yyanna laughed...

"He wanted that massage I promised him so he told his mother he was taking me home..."

"He stayed all night didn't he?" Snow asked...

"You know he did!" Yyanna laughed...

"How was that massage?" Snow asked...

"Girl – I got my lotion with the oils in it massaged him from top to bottom, and when I was done, he massaged me from inside out..."

"Ummm... what?" Snow asked...

"Basically, you get on the bed on your knees, you sit back on your legs, you lean forward, and grab the headboard. He gets behind you, he enters you, and he massages you while he's fuckin' you..."

"Damn!" They both exclaimed...

"I went to Milford on Saturday and got an extra key made..."

"See – I knew it..." Snow said...

"As soon as I got the key I ran right into Harland – I was so excited I gave him the box..."

"You put the key in a gift box?" Yyanna asked...

"Yea..."

"Aww..." Snow sighed...

"So his mother comes over and asks why does he need a key to your house if you're moving in with him?"

"Mind your fuckin' business!" Yyanna exclaimed...

"Exactly!" Snow agreed...

"So he invited me to the movies with them – and she was fuckin' pissed!" I laughed...

"I know she was – so what!" Snow laughed...

"What'd you go see?" Yyanna asked...

"The Photograph..."

"Is that good?" Snow asked...

"Yea – it's good – so he tells us he got an offer on the house and he needs to go to Fed Ex so he can print out the contract, sign it, and get it back to her – he told us to wait so I sat down – here she go following him and looking over his shoulder trying to read shit – he told her – Ma ‐ go sit back down – I'll be done in a minute – this Bitch tried to snatch the paper's off the scanner talkin' 'bout let me see that – he actually told her no!"

"Oh so he finally checked her – wow..." Snow said as she rolled her eyes..."

"Snow – when I finish telling you what happened – he's gonna make you proud..."

"He better..." Yyanna said...

"So she came over to sit by me and when he came back over to us she asked him where's the papers – he told her he shredded them..."

"That's what the fuck she get!" Snow laughed...

"Exactly!" Yyanna agreed...

"She gonna ask him why would you do that?" I laughed...

"Cause he knows his mother..." Yyanna said...

"So we go to the movies and when we get out – why does she run to the car to get in the front seat?"

"Oh my God – I can't..." Snow said... "I let Flick's mother get in the front seat – that's his mother – I'm his wife – I don't give a damn where I sit as long as I ain't gotta walk!" Snow laughed...

"Exactly..." Yyanna laughed...

"Okay – y'all ready?"

"We ready dammit!" Snow exclaimed...

"Okay... so... we get home – Harland tells the doorman to let us in the condo upstairs so he can show his mother... and baby..."

"Oh God – she didn't like it?" Yyanna asked...

"We get inside – she says what's this – he says this is your new home – she says this is a joke – right?"

"Oh no – see – that's fucked up!" Yyanna exclaimed...

"Harmony – what did he say?"

"Snow – he was so hurt – he tried not to show it – I felt so bad – he told her it wasn't a joke..."

"Dammit! What the fuck?" Snow exclaimed...

"She said you put me out my house – you sell my house out from under me – and you think I'm going to be happy here – he said yes – I thought you'd be happy here – she says why the fuck would I be happy living in an apartment when I had my own house?"

"Was it her house?" Yyanna asked...

"Before his father left, he gave the house to Harland – Harland didn't want to put his mother out so he paid all the bills and continued to let her live there..."

"So her name wasn't on the title?" Snow asked...

"No..."

"That was fucked up..."

"Harland told her it was time to let it go and she says you never asked me how I felt and he says I didn't need to ask you how you felt – you made it perfectly clear that you wanted me to continue taking care of you and continue paying all the bills in the house..."

"See – that was the problem right there..." Yyanna said...

"She tells him I brought you into this world – it's the least you can do – and he says Ma – I'm not your husband – I'm not your man – I'm your son!"

"Exactly!" Snow exclaimed...

"She says see – you let this Bitch control you – you're so knee-deep in her pussy you've lost your got-damned mind!"

"Wait one got-damned mutha fuckin' minute – Harmony you better tell me he cursed her the fuck out or I'm comin' to kick somebody's ass!"

"Well..."

"Fuck a well – did he curse her out or not?!"

"I tried to leave – he took my hand – he told me not to leave and he said first of all – I don't owe you anything – I did all that for you because I love you – second – you owe Harmony an apology for calling her out her name and disrespecting her..."

"Okay – he gets a point for that..." Yyanna said..."

"She says oh please – I call it as I see it – don't try to turn this on me – you got at least $340k for my house – you owe me $170k – and I'ma need you to run me my money so I can buy myself a house – not an apartment!"

"See – I need to come up there – she ain't apologize – he ain't curse her out – you ain't curse her out – somebody needs their ass kicked!" Snow exclaimed...

"He says first of all – you never paid a dime on that house – Dad paid the mortgage up until he left – before he left you, he left the house to me – I paid the mortgage until the house was paid off – I paid the heat, water, sewer, electric – I've been paying the taxes – and I bought you this condo - all you ever did was buy food, clothes, and weaves – so basically, I don't owe you a got-damned thing!"

"Oh!" Yyanna exclaimed...

"Wait..." Snow laughed... "He told her all she ever bought was food, clothes, and weaves – Yo! I can't!" she laughed...

"Girl – I was tryin'not to laugh!"

"She says well – you're gonna need to use that key Harmony gave you to her house – she won't be moving in because I'm not moving out – and you can sell this condo for all I care 'cause I'm not moving until you put me in a house!"

"Good – Harmony don't need to move in with him anyway..." Snow said...

"He told his mother Ma – I'm done – as soon as we close, I'm moving your things up here... I'm giving you your keys... and what you do after that is your business... he opened the door to leave she says so... that's it? You're done and we left..." I sighed...

"Wait a minute..." Yyanna said...

"When we got downstairs he punched the wall, he yelled, he broke his table, he threw a chair across the room... and the doorman banged on the door 'cause he thought Harland was beatin' my ass..."

"Oh damn!" Snow exclaimed...

"I took him over to the couch, we sat down, and he broke down crying..."

"Aww damn... I wanna cry too..." Yyanna said...

"He was telling me he tried, he did the best he could... I felt so bad y'all – I just held him and let him cry it out..."

"See – I swear – I wanna come up there and kick her ass – Flick's mother gets on my nerves but this shit here..."

"Well..."

"Oh shit..." Yyanna said...

"The doorman told us his mother left so I said why don't you move your mother's stuff upstairs while she's not here, but we hadn't closed yet so I told him to call his realtor – he called his realtor and she asked if he could move her things in – and the seller said yes!"

"Oh shit – y'all moved her shit upstairs while she was out?"

"Yes the fuck we did!" I laughed...

"Yeeesss!" Yyanna exclaimed...

"I know that's right!" Snow exclaimed...

"So we got up the next day..."

"Oh shit! You spent the night!" Yyanna exclaimed...

"I spent the night..." I sighed...

"Okay – first of all – I gotta give Harland credit – he finally checked his mother – I'm sorry he had to go through all that – but we need to drink a shot to Harland..." Snow said...

"I have a shot right here!" I exclaimed...

"I have a shot ready!" Yyanna exclaimed...

"Here's to Harland! Snow said...

"To Harland!" Yyanna and I both said as we all drank...

"So he cooked apple muffins and eggs with Swiss cheese, crumbled sausage, chopped onions, chopped peppers, and half & half cream..."

"Damn that shit sounds good!" Yyanna exclaimed...

"His mother came downstairs..."

"Oh shit – I just lost my appetite..." Snow said as she rolled her eyes..."

"She had the key I gave Harland..."

"How the fuck did she get that?" Yyanna asked...

"I guess it fell out his pocket when we were moving her things in..."

"You better hope she didn't make a copy of that shit..." Snow said...

"She better hope she didn't make a copy of that shit – I have a silent alarm and cameras..."

"Oh shit!" Yyanna exclaimed...

"So she asked what happened to the table – he told her he broke it and he was going out to buy another one – all of a sudden, she apologizes to me..."

"She apologized?" Yyanna asked...

"She said a lot happened in a short amount of time and that's no excuse, but it's all she had..."

"That's not a fuckin' excuse – that ain't no fuckin' apology!" Snow exclaimed...

"I know it's not – but I told her I accepted it anyway..."

"I don't trust her..." Yyanna said...

"I don't either..."

"So we're eating, she making small talk and Harland asks her how she likes being upstairs..."

"Oh boy..." Snow said...

"She says she likes it, it's quiet... it's comfortable..."

"She lyin'!" Yyanna laughed...

"Exactly!" Snow exclaimed...

"So she goes upstairs, we get dressed, he calls her to let her know we're ready to go – we drop her off – she says she'll call when she's ready – we go shopping – he buys another table, he buys me a secretary's desk for the office – we get in the house, Harland starts to worry because his mother didn't call... so we go check on his mother... and..." I couldn't finish... I bust out laughing...

"What the fuck happened?!" Snow exclaimed...

"We hear her fuckin' the doorman!" I laughed...

"Oh shit – what?!" Yyanna said...

"She's moanin' talkin' about it's been so long since I've had dick – give it to me!"

"Yooooo!" Snow exclaimed as we all laughed...

"We had our hands over our mouths 'cause we didn't want her to know we could hear her – and the doorman backs out the door and backs right into Harland!" I laughed...

"Oh shit – did he curse him out?"

"Naa – he told Charles he was fine with it..."

"I know that's right – he's probably happy she got some dick – maybe she'll calm the fuck down!" Snow exclaimed...

"So she comes out to see who Charles is talkin' to and see us – she gonna ask Harland what the hell are you doing here?"

"See – I'ma need Flick to hold me back – I'm comin' up there – I wanna kick her ass!" Snow exclaimed...

"Harland tells her you didn't call me to let me know to pick you up – she says Charles brought me home – and then she says well – I need to put these groceries away – I'll talk to y'all later and closes the door in our face!" I laughed...

"Harmony – does she know y'all heard her fuckin'?" Yyanna asked...

"She doesn't – but Charles does..." I laughed...

"Bitch finally got some dick – and she's still a Bitch – call him – tell him she needs some more!" Snow exclaimed...

"So I stayed Saturday night and his realtor called him Sunday morning – his closing was moved up – he closed today – and he didn't say shit to his mother!"

"Good – I wouldn't've said shit to her either!" Yyanna said...

"I'm so happy for him – his mother took horrible advantage of him – he was paying her mortgage, her bills, and his mortgage – he's going from paying $3,600 a month to $1,345 a month..."

"And that Bitch thinks he owes her money!" Snow exclaimed...

"That's why he didn't want her at the closing – she was looking to get paid..." Yyanna said...

"I told him I want him to take me out tonight to celebrate – but I don't want to spend the night there – I want to go home..."

"Harmony – why?"

"We can continue the celebration at my house..."

"Harmony? What's going on?"

"I'm moving in with him..." I sighed...

"I knew it!" Snow exclaimed...

"I wasn't going to – I like having my own – but he bought me that desk..."

"So all it took was a desk?" Yyanna asked...

"Well... I said if I moved in with him we'd need a bigger place because he doesn't have enough room for my office, my clothes, etc... one thing led to another..." I sighed...

"Would you really move in with him?" Snow asked...

"I would consider moving into our place – in our name..."

"I know that's right!" Yanna said...

"Alright y'all – It's 10 minutes after – I gotta head back – I'll keep you posted..."

"Alright – bye!" they both said as they left the room...

Chapter 28

"Good morning..." Harland greeted as he walked into his attorney's office..."

"Good morning..." they all said in unison...

"I'm Harland Wilkins..." he said as he sat down..."

"I'm Sheddi Lemdon, Harland's Realtor..."

"I'm Beverly Carswell, Harland's attorney..."

"I'm Attorney Heche, I represent the seller..."

"I'm Raymond Johnson, I'm the realtor for the seller..."

"Nice meeting you all..." Beverly said as she took out a folder... " This is going to be a fast one – my client has already signed a lot of the papers – Harland, you'll need to sign and date all of these – I've indicated where you need to sign and date them – you'll receive a copy of the entire package before you leave..." she said as she took the papers out the folder and pushed them over to Harland and then she continued... "Okay – you sold your property located at 1266 Laurel Avenue in Bridgeport for $340 thousand – out of that $340 thousand, you purchased a 1 bed, 1 bath condo for $94 thousand located at 881 Lafayette Blvd, Unit 2J in Bridgeport – is that correct?"

"That's correct..." Harland acknowledged...

"Okay Raymond – here's the check for $94 thousand..."

"Thank you..." Raymond said as he took the check...

"Okay – we also received a pay-off statement of $190 thousand for your property located at 881 Lafayette Blvd, Unit 1B in Bridgeport – is that correct?"

"That's correct..." Harland acknowledged...

"Okay – here's the check – it's dated for today – after you sign these papers, the check will be mailed to them..."

"Thank you..."

"Okay – your realtor gets 6 percent commission of the sale of your home – that's $20,400..."

"That's correct..." Harland acknowledged...

"Here's your check Sheddi..." Beverly said as she handed her the check..."

"Thank you..." Sheddi said...

"Okay – your realtor also gets 3 percent commission of the sale of the condo you purchased – that's $2,820..." Raymond said...

"That's correct..." Sheddi acknowledged...

"Here's your check..." Raymond said as he handed it to her..."

"Thank you..."

"Okay – my fees are $9,600..." Beverly said...

"That's correct..." Harland acknowledged...

"Here's my check..." she said as she showed it to him... "It'll be deposited later today..."

"You're welcome..." Harland said as everyone laughed..."

"Okay – you sold your home, you purchased another home, you paid off your current mortgage, you paid your realtor, and you paid me – now it's time to pay you..." Beverly said as she handed him a check for $26,000...

"Thank you..." he sighed...

"You're welcome..." Harland put the check in his pocket and they all sat there as he finished signing the papers. When he was done, he put the pen down on the table... "We're all set – it's been a pleasure!" Beverly exclaimed as she stood up. Harland stood up along with everyone else, they all shook hands, and then Raymond and Attorney Heche left...

"Harland, do you need me to stay?" Sheddi asked...

"Naa – I'm good..."

"Okay – congratulations – I'll see you later..." she said as she left. Harland sat there and waited a few minutes and then Beverly came out with an envelope...

"Here you go – congratulations again..."

"Thank you..." Harland said as he got up, shook her hand, and then he left...

"Le'me see who this is..." Sheddi said as she looked at her phone... "Ms. Wilkins – our business has been concluded – you can speak to your son if you have any questions..." she said out loud as she tossed her phone in the seat beside her, let the call go to voicemail, and drove off...

"Ms. Lemdon – this is Helen Wilkins – I'm just calling to confirm the date and time for next week – I'd like to be at the closing – please call me back..."

Chapter 29

"Hey..." I sighed as I answered...

"Hey... can you talk?"

"Not really – I just got back from lunch..."

"Can you call me back?"

"I'll put you on blue tooth so I can work..." I said as I connected the blue tooth and turned on my computer... "Okay – I'm up..."

"How was your day?"

"I spent the bulk of my lunch hour talking about you..."

"Oh so you've been talking about me?"

"Yea..."

"Do I know them?"

"I met them in Facebook..."

"They have your phone number?"

"I have a room..."

"You have a room?"

"Yes – you know what Facebook live is?"

"Yes..."

"Well the room is private – the only people in the room are the ones you invite..."

"Do you invite men into this room?"

"I only invite women – but Snow's husband pops in from time to time..."

"Oh so they're married..."

"Snow & Yyanna are married..."

"Do you ever go live?"

"Sometimes – but I don't go live when I'm in the room..."

"So... what do you talk about?"

"We talk about everything..."

"Do you talk about sex?"

"Absolutely..."

"You said Snow's husband pops in sometimes..."

"I met Snow on her lives – we've always been friends in Facebook but since I've started watching her lives, I'm friends with her husband too..."

"Oh so her husband participates in the lives with her?"

"Yea..."

"You said he pops in your room sometimes..."

"Snow works from home – if I see her husband I'll tell him hello, or he'll pop in to give his opinion..."

"I see... so what is his opinion of me?"

"His opinion doesn't matter..."

"It matters to me..."

"Well... basically he wants me to be sure I know what I'm doing – he wants you to be the man for me..."

"So you've been asking him for advice..."

"No – I've been venting to Snow and Yyanna – one day Flick overheard me telling them about me ridding your dick so he started eavesdropping – when I started to vent, he popped in to give me his opinion..."

"So... you told them you ride my dick..."

"We talk about everything..."

"And he was listening..."

"Yea..."

"Interesting..."

"Are you upset?"

"I'm not upset – I just find it interesting that he was listening to you talk about ridding my dick..."

"When I started watching their lives, they had a bet going..."

"A bet?"

"Yes – the one who lasted the longest would win..."

"Are you saying they had sex on their live?"

"No!" I laughed... "They had a bet to see how many nights they could go before someone tapped out..."

"Oh... okay..."

"Every night we would watch their live and they would tell us what happened the night before..."

"On Facebook?"

"Snow has a private page for the lives – only friends can see – the lives don't go on her main page..."

"Oh – I get it – now I understand why you ladies talk the way you do – and I also understand why he was eavesdropping..."

"So you're not upset..."

"No – I'm not upset – but I want to ask you something – and I want you to be honest..."

"Okay..."

"Did you talk about my mother?"

"Yea..."

"I'm sorry..."

"For what?"

"I didn't realize it was affecting you to that extent..."

"I waited a long time. When I told them about you they were happy for me..."

"Are they still happy for you?"

"They were always happy for me - but when I started venting to them, they became really concerned..."

"I can understand that..."

"I told them everything that's been going on..."

"I figured that..."

"They're happy for you..."

"They're happy for me?"

"I told them everything – they're happy that you were able to sell your house, pay off your mortgage, pay off your mother's mortgage, etc..."

"I want to meet them..."

"I can introduce you..."

"I wish you didn't have to tell them about my mother..."

"I'm sorry – I love you – but it's hard – talking to them kept me sane..."

"I'm sorry – after today, I'm going to do my best to make it up to you – I love you..."

"I love you too..."

"I know you do – you wouldn't have put up with all this if you didn't..."

"What time are you picking me up tonight?"

"I'll be at the train at 6 – unless you get there earlier..."

"Make it 5:30 – I'm gonna try and get the 4:12 I Bus so I can catch the 5:07 express out of Stamford..."

"I'll be there at 5:30..."

"How did everything go today?"

"It was great – but I'll talk to you about that tonight..."

"Okay – I'll see you later..."

"See you later..."

"I love you..."

"I love you too..."

Chapter 30

"Hey!" I exclaimed as I hurried over to Harland..."

"Hey!" he laughed as he hugged me tight and picked me up off the ground... "C'mon..." he said as he took my hand and pulled me across the street...

"Where are we going?"

"Get in!" he commanded...

"Okay!" Harland started the car and I looked out the window. I thought we were going to Stratford at first, but then I realized we were going to Shelton... "Where are we going?" Harland didn't answer me – he just smiled and kept on driving. When I saw where we were going, I got really excited... "Longhorn Steak House!"

"Yes..." he answered as he parked the car...

"Thank you, thank you, thank you, thank you, thank you!" I exclaimed as I kissed him over and over and over...

"You're welcome..." he laughed... "Let's go inside..."

"Okay!" I squealed as I opened the door and got out before he could open the door for me...

"You just can't let me be a gentleman..." he laughed...

"I'll let you open that door for me..." I said as I took his hand...

"Let me? Okay then..." he laughed as we went inside...

"Table for two?" the hostess asked...

"Yes..." Harland answered...

"Really?" I asked...

"My mother's not here..."

"She's not here yet..."

"Harmony – I haven't seen my mother all day..."

"Hmmm – maybe she's getting comfortable in her new place..."

"Maybe..." he agreed as we followed the hostess to our table and sat down...

"Oh Charles... Yes..."

"Helen... Helen... Helen..."

"Don't stop Charles..."

"I won't Baby... I won't..."

"Welcome to Longhorn Steakhouse – can I start you off with something to drink?" the waitress asked...

"I'll have a margarita..." I said...

"I'll have a Pepsi..."

"You're not drinking?" I asked...

"I have to drive..."

"I'll be right back..." the waitress said and then she left...

"I have something to tell you..." I said...

"Okay – tell me..."

"When I was talking to Snow and Yyanna this afternoon..."

"Here's your drinks – are you ready to order?" the waitress interrupted...

"I want the seasoned steakhouse wings with blue cheese and fried shrimp with steakhouse mac & cheese..."

"I'll have the renegade sirloin with red rock grilled shrimp and the loaded baked potato..."

"Okay – I'll be back..." the waitress said and then she went to place our order...

"Now..." he said as he took my hands... "Where were we?"

"I told them I was thinking about moving in with you..."

"Harmony... do you mean that?"

"Yes..." Harland got up from his seat, came over to sit beside me, pulled me into a kiss, and kissed me hard...

"I have something to show you..." he said as he took an envelope out his jacket and handed it to me..."

"Harland! Congratulations!"

"It's yours..."

"Harland... No... I can't..."

"Yes..." he breathed as he kissed me... "You can..." he breathed as he kissed me again and I started crying...

"I love you so much..."

"I love you too..." he said as he picked up his drink and picked up mine so I could take it...

"Here's to us..."

"To us..." I said as we clinked and took a gulp...

"I want you to put that money on your mortgage..."

"Okay..." I sniffed...

"You're serious about moving in with me – right?"

"Yes Harland – but we need to talk about that..."

"Here's your food – are you staying over here?" the waitress asked Harland...

"Naa – I'm about to get it in – I need elbow room..." he laughed as he got up and went to sit back across from me... "Damn this looks good..." he breathed...

"It sure does – let's start with the chicken wings..."

"Okay – but you said we need to talk..." he said as we both took a wing and started eating...

"I don't want to move into your place – it's too small..."

"Would you rather I move in with you?"

"I want to sell my house, I want you to sell your condo, and we get a place together..."

"I like being downtown – you like the suburbs – how are we going to compromise?"

"I was thinking maybe we could move to Black Rock..."

"Black Rock?"

"Yea – it's closer to downtown than where I live now..."

"True – but I can walk to work – I won't be able to do that if I move to Black Rock..."

"That's true..."

"We'll come up with something..."

"I already came up with something..." I said as I passed him my phone to read the following:

1,512 Sq. Ft.
Gas Fireplace
Private Balcony
Walk-In-Closet,
Master Suite with Master Bath
33 North Water Street, South Norwalk, CT
$580k – Mortgage $3,600
Taxes $724
HOA $728

Harland took one look at it and bust out laughing... "Oh wow!"

"Umm... what's so funny?"

"The mortgage..." he laughed... "It's $3,600 a month!"

"Oh shit – I didn't even realize that..."

"I went from paying $3,600 a month..." he laughed... "To $3,600 a month..." He laughed again... "And now I'm going right back to $3,600 a month! Aaaa Haaah! Aaaaa Haaah!"

"I don't know if I should be mad you're laughing... or happy you're laughing..."

"Don't be mad... I can't help it..." he laughed...

"Well stop laughing then!" I laughed. We sat at the table laughing for about 15 minutes. I'd stop, he'd start, and we'd be laughing again...

"Okay Harland – I need to get serious for a minute..."

"Okay..."

"I love it..."

"It's nice... but it's in South Norwalk..."

"I know..."

"I can't walk to work..."

"I'll be home sooner..."

"That's true..."

"We have a gas fireplace..."

"I know..."

"We have a balcony..."

"I know..."

"We have a walk-in closet..."

"I know..."

"It's perfect for us..."

"Harmony – it's five hundred eighty thousand dollars..."

"I know..." I sighed...

"How's everything going?" the waitress asked...

"Good..." Harland answered...

"Would you like any dessert?"

"We have dessert waiting for us at home..." he answered as he smiled at me mischievously...

"Okay then – here's your check – you can pay at the table or pay on your way out..." she said before she walked away. Harland took out his credit card, paid the check, and we got up to leave...

Harland closed the door, locked it, and set the alarm...

"Come here..." he commanded as he pulled me into his arms and kissed me hard...

"Mmmph..." I moaned as he pushed his tongue in my mouth...

"C'mon..." he said as he took my hand and led me upstairs. It happened so fast I don't even remember getting undressed...

"Harland... Fuck... Don't stop... I'm cumming!"

"I'm cummin' with you... I'm cummin' with you..."

"Aaahh...   Aaahh...   Aaahh...   Aaahh... Aaahhh!!"

"Uggh!   Uggh!   Uggh!   Uggh! Uuuggghhh!!"

Harland was still lying between my legs when Siri began singing her song to wake us up for work...

"Good morning Mr. Wilkins..." Charles greeted as Harland came into the lobby...

"Good morning..."

"Harland – I was just about to call you – when is the closing on the house?" Helen asked as she came out of the deli...

"Mom – let's talk inside..."

"Okay – I'll see you later Charles..." she said as she followed Harland and they went inside... "I left a message with Sheddi – she hasn't called me back – I want to be there..." she said as she sat down...

"Ma – the closing happened yesterday..."

"Yesterday? Why the fuck didn't you tell me?"

"Why the fuck did I need to tell you?"

"Excuse me?"

"I didn't stutter – why the fuck did I need to tell you?"

"That was my house – you owe me..."

"Ma – we already had this discussion – I paid off the house – not you – Dad left the house to me – not you – and I bought you a condo – stop acting like you're homeless!"

"You didn't want me there because you don't want me to know how much money you got!"

"You already know how much money I got! You're just mad because I didn't give you any!"

"I bet you gave that Bitch some money – I bet she was at the closing too – that's the real reason you didn't want me there – isn't it?" Harland went to his door and opened it...

"GET OUT!"

"You're putting me out?" Harland went over to the couch, lifted his mother up by her arm, pulled her towards the door, pushed her out in the hallway, and slammed the door...

"UUUGGGHHHH!" he exclaimed as he punched the wall...

"Mutha fucka think he can treat me like this and I won't do shit – guess again – you gon' learn taday – you both are!" Helen exclaimed as she left the building...

"Good afternoon Ms. Thompson..." the manager said as he came over to me...

"Good afternoon – I need to make a deposit..." I said as I got up...

"I'm sure one of our tellers can help you..."

"No – they can't..."

"Come with me..." he said as I followed him into his office... "How can I help you?"

"I want to deposit this check – and then I want to put it on my mortgage..." I answered as I handed him the check...

"Do you pay your mortgage on line?"

"Yes..."

"Okay – we'll deposit the check for you – you can make your payment on line today – normally it takes 48 hours to process but if it comes in tonight we'll honor it..."

"I won't get a fee for being over-drawn?"

"No – I'll make a note in the account – just sign here..."

"Okay..." I said as I signed the check...

"I'll be right back..." he said as he went to do the deposit... "You're all set..." he said as he came back into the office and handed me the deposit slip... "You can go online at the terminal and make your payment..."

"Thank you Kevin..."

"You're welcome Ms. Thompson – have a good day..."

"Thank you..." I said as I got up. I went over to the terminal, logged in, made my payment, and went to get something to eat... "I'm going to take this back to work..." I said out loud as I walked towards my building. I got to my desk, took off my coat, took out my lunch, and just as I was about to start eating, I got an alert on my phone... "Hmmm – I wonder if he decided to go home for lunch..." I asked out loud as I looked at my phone... "I love looking at you on camera..." I sighed as I opened the camera. I looked at the screen and I was mortified. I started crying as I watched his mother open my closet and run her hand across my lingerie... "What the fuck is she doing in my house?!" I exclaimed as I called Harland...

"Hey!"

"Harland!" I cried...

"Harmony – what's wrong?"

"Your mother!"

"Oh my God – is she alright?"

"She's in my house!"

"What?!"

"She broke in my house – she's in the bedroom – I'm on my way home..."

"I'll meet you there!"

"Is everything alright?" my supervisor asked as she came out her office...

"No – somebody broke into my house – I need to leave!" I exclaimed as I got up, snatched my pocketbook, snatched my coat, and flew out the door... "I need to get an uber..." I breathed. I ordered the uber as tears streamed down my face. When the uber got there, the driver seemed concerned...

"Are you okay?"

"I'm fine – thanks for asking..." I answered as I sat down, closed the door, and looked at the camera. I watched in horror as his mother tried on the set I bought to surprise him with later that night. She admired herself in the mirror and posed in front of the mirror as she turned to look at her ass... "Fuckin' Bitch!" I exclaimed as she took off my lingerie, hung it back on the hanger, and took out another one to try on...

"We're here Maam..." the driver said...

"Thank you..." I responded as I got out. I waited for the driver to drive off before I opened the door and went inside. Thank God our alarm is silent because she didn't realize that I was in the house. I reset the alarm so I would get another recording and when I saw what she was doing next, my mouth dropped open...

"Ooohhh... this is big!" I heard her exclaim as she pulled the 9-inch strap-on dildo out the nightstand drawer... "I bet he fucks her good with this..." she laughed as she stepped into it. I began smiling to myself as I crept upstairs, clicked on Facebook, and went live...

"Hello Helen..." I greeted as I walked into my bedroom...

"I see you like big dicks..." she replied as she turned to face me and started shaking the dick in her hand...

"That's your son's dick…" I lied as I continued recording…

"This isn't my son's dick – it's yours! And when I leave here, I'm going to tell everyone I know! I told you – you'll never be rid of me – you'll never beat me!"

"You might wanna wash your hands…" I laughed… "I forgot to clean it after I fucked your son in the ass last night…" I lied…

"You're lying! My son would never!"

"He'd never admit it…" I laughed… "But he loves it…"

"We'll see about that!" she gritted

"You might wanna get dressed…"

"I'll get dressed when I'm ready – you know what – on second thought – I'm not getting dressed – you should just give me this outfit – it looks better on me anyway…"

"You can have it – I don't think the police will mind…" I said as I stopped the live, posted it to Facebook, and left the bedroom…

"Police? You're having me arrested?"

"I sure am…" I said as I started downstairs…

"You might wanna reconsider…" she said as she came downstairs and sat beside me…

"You broke in my house – I didn't invite you here…" I said as I dialed 911…

"911 – what's your emergency?"

"I have an intruder in my house…"

"I'm not an intruder!" Helen snapped…

"Maam? Is she there in the house with you?"

"I never invited her – she broke in my house and she's refusing to leave..."

"You won't get away with this..." Helen hissed...

"Maam – we're sending the police..."

"Thank you..." I said before hanging up...

"My son will take care of this!" she said as she got up and went towards the door...

"Leaving so soon?" I asked sarcastically as Harland unlocked the door and came inside...

"What the hell is going on here?" he exclaimed...

"Thank God you're here – she called the police on me!" Helen exclaimed as she ran over to Harland...

"Harmony – what the fuck..."

"You and your mother are not welcome here – please leave!"

"Harmony – wait..."

"I'm done waiting! Your mother broke in, went upstairs, went through my lingerie, went in the nightstand, and put on the strap on you like me to fuck you in the ass with – you and she need to get the fuck out! Now!"

"You heard her!" Sergeant Corbett said as he came inside...

"I want to press charges..." I said as I stood up...

"Maam – you're under arrest..."

"Sir wait – Harmony – please..."

"I have a key!" Helen exclaimed. Everyone stopped and looked at her...

"Where's your key?" Sergeant Corbett asked as the other officer looked on...

"It's upstairs with my clothes..." she sighed...

"Upstairs with your clothes?!" Harland exclaimed...

"Maam – did you give her a key to your home?" the officer asked...

"Hell no!"

"I'm sorry – you need to come with us..." the officer said as he began to escort Helen towards the front door...

"Harmony – if you do this – I'm done!" Harland exclaimed...

"Bye!" I said as I waived at them both...

"Ma – I'm sorry..." Harland sighed as he followed the officer, his mother, and Sergeant Corbett out the door...

I threw myself on the couch and cried like a baby...

Chapter 32

"No please – please don't put me in there!" Helen pleaded...

"Ms. Wilkins – don't make this any harder than it has to be!" the officer snapped...

"You don't have to treat her like that!" Harland exclaimed...

"Mr. Wilkins – come with me..." Sergeant Corbett commanded...

"I'M NOT GOING ANYWHERE WITH YOU UNTIL YOU TELL ME WHAT'S GOING ON WITH MY MOTHER!"

"Mr. Wilkins – I'm trying to be nice – I know you work for the court – I need you to come with me – please!"

"FINE!" Harland boomed as he followed Sergeant Corbett into his office...

"First – I'm sorry..."

"I don't wanna hear it..."

"You really think I wanna do this?!"

"Honestly? Hell yea!"

"Mr. Wilkins!"

"That's my mother..." he said as he broke down...

"I know man... I know..." Sergeant Corbett said as he got up, went over to Harland, and put his hand on his shoulder...

"Can she come home?"

"I'm sorry – she has to stay here for the night – it's after 5 – but she'll see the judge first thing tomorrow morning..."

"I can't leave my mother in jail!"

"I'm sorry..."

"Can I see her?"

"She has to be processed – once she's processed – you can see her..."

"Ms. Wilkins – you need to remove your clothes..." Gert said...

"I'm wearing a night gown!"

"I understand that – but you need to remove your clothes and put on this orange jumpsuit..." she said as she handed it to Helen...

"Turn around!"

"I'm sorry Ms. Wilkins – I can't do that..."

"FINE!" she yelled as she took off the gown and put on the jump suit... "Happy now?"

"Hell yea – I get to go home..." she answered as she pushed Helen in the cell, locked it, and left with the night gown...

"Has Ms. Wilkins been processed?" Sergeant Corbett asked...

"Yes sir..." Gert answered as she swiped her I.D., clocked out, and left the precinct...

"Mr. Wilkins – come with me..." Sergeant Corbett said as he motioned for Harland to get up and follow him...

"Ma!" he exclaimed as he ran over to the cell...

"Harland – don't leave me in here – please..."

"I'm sorry Ma – I can't get you out until tomorrow..."

"You work for the fuckin' courthouse and you can't get me outta here?!"

"Ma – I can't deal with this right now..." he said as he left. When he got outside, he broke down again...

"Mutha fucka gonna leave me in jail – he's the one that should be in here – he took everything away from me..." she mumbled as she saw a piece of the threading was loose on the bottom bunk and began pulling it...

"What the fuck is wrong with her?" the male officer laughed...

"Hell if I know – or care..." the other officer laughed...

"You think we should go check on her?"

"For what? She doesn't have anything but the orange jump suit – she's not even wearing shoes!"

"Yea – you're right – she'll be alright for a couple of hours..."

"I got something for all you mutha fuckas!" Helen mumbled as she finished pulling the threading from around the bottom bunk... "I'd rather die than spend the night in here..." she mumbled as she tied the threading into a noose, tied it to the top bunk, slipped the noose around her neck, tightened it, slid down towards the floor, and began to lose consciousness...

"Good night Sarge..." the officers said...

"How's Ms. Wilkin's doing?"

"She's been quiet for about 4 hours..." one of them answered...

"When was the last time you check on her?"

"We haven't – she was doing a lot of mumbling when she first got in there but once she got quiet, we figured she was sleep..."

"Did you clock out yet?"

"No Sarge..."

"Good – wait here – I'll be right back..."

"Why the fuck didn't you lie and say we checked on her?" the other officer snapped...

"CALL THE PARAMEDICS!" Sergeant Corbett yelled...

"Sarge – what's wrong?"

"SHE'S DEAD!!"

Chapter 33

"In here!" Sergeant Corbett exclaimed as the paramedics came in...

"How long has she been in here?" one of the paramedics asked...

"She came in a little after 5..."

"We'll get her body to the coroner – has the family been notified?"

"No..." Sergeant Corbett sighed...

"We're going to need someone to claim the body..."

"Her name is Helen Wilkins..." Sergeant Corbett sighed as they took Helen's body out on the stretcher, put it on the ambulance, and drove off...

"Hey Chandler..." Starr sighed...
"Hey..."

"What's wrong?"

"I can't talk about it..."

"Are you coming home?"

"I can't..."

"What can I do?"

"Talk to me – I need to hear your voice..."

"The kids are still up – you want me to get them?"

"No..."

"Okay..."

"How was dinner?"

"I didn't eat yet..."

"Why?"

"I wanted to have dinner with you..."

"You didn't eat anything?"

"I made spaghetti – I had a couple of meatballs..."

"Are the kids behaving themselves?"

"Yea..."

"Why aren't they in bed?"

"They are – they've been in bed since 10..."

"And they're still up?"

"Yea..." she laughed...

"Call your mother and tell her you love her..."

"I will..."

"I love you Starr..."

'I love you too Chandler..."

"Make sure you get some sleep..."

"Do you plan on waking me up?"

"I might..."

"We have a suicide..." one of the paramedics said as they wheeled Helen's body in..."

"I'll get the doctor..." the nurse said as she got up... "Doctor – we have a suicide..."

'I'll be right there..." the doctor said as he got up and went over to the paramedics... "Do you have an approximate time of death?" he asked...

"The Sergeant told us she was brought in after 5..."

"So between 5pm and midnight – okay – we need to get the coroner down here to take her to the morgue..." the doctor said and then he went to get the coroner. When Mr. Grady got to the E.R., he took Helen's body down to the morgue and began his examination after he turned on his recorder...

"The deceased, Helen Wilkins, arrived here on Wednesday, February 10th, at 12:30 a.m. Sometime between the hours of 5 p.m. on Tuesday, February 9th, and Midnight on Wednesday, February 10th, the deceased died from self-inflicted brain hypoxia, which was caused by a lack of oxygen to the brain. The deceased has a deep mark around her neck, supporting the cause of death. The position of the mark around her neck and the angle of the mark going up and behind the neck do not indicate or suggest that the deceased was murdered...

"Hey Chandler..."

"I need your help Jeremy..."

"What happened?"

"Harland Wilkins..."

"Oh my God – is he dead?"

"His mother..."

"No! What happened?"

"We responded to a call at his girlfriend's house..."

"The girlfriend killed his mother?"

"She called 911 and said his mother broke in – when we got there, she wanted to press charges..."

"What – why – I don't get it – if she's dating Harland, why would she have his mother arrested?"

"She claims his mother wasn't invited..."

"Was she?"

"She has surveillance – his mother broke in – with a key..."

"She had a key? And the girlfriend still pressed charges?"

"The girlfriend said she didn't give the mother a key..."

"Chandler – I'm confused – why didn't she just ask her to leave?"

"She did – his mother refused to leave..."

"Did she really break in or is this woman being vengeful and vindictive?"

"We watched the surveillance – she let herself in, she went upstairs to the bedroom – when Harmony went upstairs she asked her what she was doing in the house – she told the woman I'm calling the police – it seems as if his mother was being vengeful and vindictive..."

"Why?"

"From what I saw and heard on the surveillance – his mother has issues..."

"Chandler – I need you to spell it out..."

"Can't you just come here and help me?"

"Yes Chandler – I'm on my way..."

"Harmony – what the fuck?!" Snow asked...

"Girl – I'm glad you came in the room – you must not be going to work!" Yyanna laughed...

"I'm glad I'm in here too..." I said as I lit my blunt and started smoking as I started crying...

"Harmony – see – I'ma have Flick bring me up there – I'm done – I'm fuckin' done!" Snow exclaimed...

"Harmony – does Harland know you put his mother on live?"

"No..." I answered as I continued smoking and crying...

"Take it down – you don't need to have it on Facebook – you need to give it to the police – her ass needs to be in jail!" Snow exclaimed...

"Baby what's goin' on?" Flick asked as he came in...

"Flick – I need you to take me up there – some shit went down with his mother..."

"I'm not takin' you up there – last thing I need is for you to wind up in jail – nope – Harmony – you good – oh shit – what the fuck – why you cryin' – he did something to you?"

"No..." I cried...

"Y'all broke up?"

"Yea..." I sniffed as I finished my blunt...

"See – if he was the man for you – you wouldn't be cryin' right now – you gon' be alright though – you gon' meet somebody that deserves you..."

"Thank you Flick..."

"You don't have to thank me..." he said as he went in the kitchen...

"Snow – tell Flick to come back – I want him to hear this..."

"Flick – Harmony said come back – she wants you to hear this..."

"Aiight – I'm comin'..."

"Harland sold his house. On Monday, he went to the closing. He wanted me to come but I told him if I go we'll both catch hell so I went to work..."

'I would 'a went to work too..." Yyanna said...

"Harland picked me up from the train and we went to Longhorn Steakhouse – I told him I was thinking about moving in with him..."

"No, no, no!" Flick exclaimed...

"Let her finish Babe..." Snow said...

"I told him I wanted us to buy a place together..."

"I don't think you should do it..." Flick said...

"This was before they broke up..." Snow said...

"Even if they was still together – I don't think you should do it..." Flick said...

"So I found a place in South Norwalk that might work for both of us..."

"Uh huh..." Flick said as he gave me the side eye..."

"Harland sold his house, he paid off his mortgage, paid off his mother's condo, paid the realtor, paid the attorney, and after it was all said and done, he got a check for $26,000..."

"Oh wow – he must 'a got a lot of money for his house..." Yyanna said...

"When we were at dinner he..." I couldn't finish... I started crying again...

"What happened?" Flick asked, concerned...

"He gave me the check..."

"What?!" they all exclaimed...

"He told me to take the money and put it on my mortgage..." I cried...

"Damn – I ain't never had a man give me money towards my mortgage..." Yyanna said...

"Flick – if that was you – would you have given me that check?" Snow asked...

"Nope – I would 'a bought you a ring, I would 'a proposed and we would 'a got married without a pre-nup ⁻ so you'd get my money anyway..." he answered as he started kissing on her neck...

"You stupid!" Snow laughed...

"Harmony – did you put that money on your mortgage already?" Yyanna asked...

"I went to the bank this afternoon and had the manager put a note in my account so even if it takes two days to clear – it goes on my mortgage tonight..."

"Harmony – it seems like he really loves you – but you cryin' – y'all broke up – what happened?" Flick asked...

"Snow – show him the live..." I watched Flick's eyes bulge before he put his hand over his mouth...

"That's his mother?!"

"Yea..."

"Yo – that Bitch is crazy!" he said and then he bust out laughing... "Does he know you put this in Facebook?"

"I don't think so..."

"Take it down before he sees it..."

"He's gonna see it even if I take it down..."

"How? Somebody downloaded it?"

"The police have it…"

"The police have it? How did they get it?"

"She broke in my house – she tripped the alarm – everything was recorded…"

"Oh shit! Did you press charges?"

"Yea…" I answered as I started crying again…

"Wait – does he know his mother did this?"

"I called him – he was here when the cops got here – he said if I press charges we're done…"

"Oh hell no – fuck him – I see why my wife wanna come up there!"

"She told the cops she didn't break in 'cause she had a key…"

"I knew she was gonna copy that key!" Snow exclaimed…

"Wait – he gave his mother a key to your house?"

"No – when she was out the other day we moved her things in – he dropped it – she found it and brought it back to him…"

"And she made herself a copy before she brought it back…" Snow said…

"Why the fuck didn't he put the fuckin' key on his key ring?" Flick asked…

"I put it in a gift box…"

"So what? You open the box –you take out your key – you put it on your key ring – if he had put it on his key ring, she would 'a never got a hold of it…"

"I agree with Flick…" Yyanna said…

"I don't know what to do..." I sighed...

"Harmony – don't feel bad – you did what you were supposed to do..." Flick said...

"What if he tries to get his money back?" Snow asked...

"He gave her that check – he told her to put it on her mortgage – that's on him..." Flick answered...

"Exactly..." Yyanna agreed...

"Alright y'all – I'ma go try and get some sleep..."

"You goin' to work?"

"No... Ima take the rest of the week..."

"Good – let us know what happened..." Snow said...

"I will..." I said as we left the room...

"Le'me take this live down..." I said as I went to my page and took it down. Unfortunately, I didn't bother to look and see who already saw it...

"I'm Della Crews, Anchor, News 12 Connecticut. We interrupt our regularly scheduled programming to bring you the following news. We now go live to Gwen Edwards. Go ahead Gwen...

"This is Gwen Edwards, Reporter, News 12 Connecticut. We're live at the First Precinct in Bridgeport. Earlier this morning, we were informed that a female inmate has committed suicide. The inmate was arrested for breaking and entering on Tuesday evening and was scheduled to go before Judge Duffey later today. At this time, the name of the inmate is not being released. We'll continue to bring you updates..."

"Oh God... Please... No..." Harland I both said in unison...

"Who is it?" Harland asked as he got up to go see who'd be knocking at his door after 2 a.m...."

"It's Sergeant Corbett..."

"What the hell are you doing..." Harland snatched the door open and when he saw Sergeant Hurley, he broke down...

"I gotchu..." Sergeant Corbett said as he helped Harland up...

"My mother's dead?"

"Yes Harland – I'm sorry..."

"Who are you?" he asked as he turned to Sergeant Hurley..."

"I'm Sergeant Hurley – I would out in Milford..."

"I thought I recognized you..."

"You work in the courthouse – right?"

"Yea..."

"I'm sorry we had to meet under these circumstances..."

"So am I..." Harland sighed...

"We need you to come down to the coroner's office to identify the body..."

"How did my mother die?"

"We'll talk about that when we get to the hospital..." Sergeant Corbett answered...

"No – we're going to talk about it right now!"

"Can we come in?" Sergeant Hurley asked...

"Come in..."

"Your mother committed suicide..." Sergeant Corbett answered...

"What?! How the hell was she able to do that? She wasn't even wearing shoes! You have her clothes! Oh my God Ma – Whhyyy?" he cried as he broke down again and Sergeant Hurley caught him before he hit the floor... "How?" he asked again...

"The threading around the mattress on the bottom bunk was loose..."

"Threading?"

"It held the mattress together... she pulled it... tied it... and..."

"Are you sure my mother wasn't murdered?"

"Harland – you know better than that..."

"Don't tell me what the fuck I know! Right now – I know my mother's dead!"

"Mr. Wilkins – if I may say something?" Sergeant Hurley asked...

"Go 'head!"

"The precincts have cameras in the corridors where the holding cells are – we've reviewed the footage – none of the officers went anywhere near her cell – there were no other inmates in holding – she wasn't murdered..."

"So nobody went to check on my mother?"

"No..." Sergeant Corbett sighed...

"How long was my mother dead before anybody realized she was dead?"

"I went to check on your mother at midnight..."

"Midnight?! You mean to tell me my mother was in her cell for 7 hours before you knew she was dead?!"

"Yes..."

"It's after 2 a.m. – why wasn't I called?"

"Protocol dictates..." Sergeant Harley started to say...

"Man – fuck protocol – why am I just now finding out my mother is dead?!"

"When an inmate dies, we have to get them to the coroner to determine the cause of death before we notify the family..."

"You could 'a called me!"

"We couldn't... I'm sorry..." Sergeant Corbett said...

"I want to see the surveillance – and those officers better be fired for not doing their got-damned jobs!"

"We'll take you to the precinct as soon as we leave the coroner's office...

"I'm going to take back the sheet now..." Mr. Grady said...

"I'm ready..." Harland sighed... "Ma..." he whispered as he started crying... "Wait!" he exclaimed as he grabbed Mr. Grady's wrist. Sergeant Hurley had his hand on his gun and Sergeant Corbett motioned for him to relax before Harland had a chance to notice... "I love you..."

Harland said as he kissed his mother on her forehead, pulled up the sheet, and went out into the hallway...

"Come with me..." Sergeant Corbett said as they walked back into the precinct...

"You still need me Chandler?" Sergeant Hurley asked...

"I'm good Jeremy – thank you..."

"You're welcome..." he said as he left and Harland went into the office with Sergeant Corbett...

"Have a seat..." Sergeant Corbett said. Harland sat next to him, Sergeant Corbett opened a laptop, and pulled up the surveillance... "This is your mother entering the house..."

"I know..." Harland acknowledged as the continued to watch...

"This is where your girlfriend confronts her..."

"Harmony..." Harland whispered...

"And his is her Facebook page..."

"Why are you showing me her Facebook page?"

"Because... when she confronted your mother... she went live on Facebook..."

"What?!"

"Yes..."

"Hold on..." Harland said as he went to my page but failed to see it because it's friends only...

"It's not there anymore – she took it down – but it was there earlier..."

"I know she was mad – she had a right to be mad – but Facebook?"

"Your mother had a key to her house – she let herself in – she taunted your girlfriend..."

"My mother is manic-depressive..."

"Does your girlfriend know this?"

"Yes..."

"I hope you can find it in your heart to forgive her..."

"Forgive her? My mother's dead because of her!"

"Harland – I know you're upset... but..."

"I begged her not to press charges – I was going to take care of it – now my mother's dead – and so are we!" he said as he got up and left...

"I'm Della Crews, Anchor, News 12 Connecticut. We interrupt our regularly scheduled programming to bring you the following news. We now go live to Gwen Edwards. Go ahead Gwen...

"This is Gwen Edwards, Reporter, News 12 Connecticut. Earlier this morning, we were informed that a female inmate has committed suicide. The inmate was arrested for breaking and entering on Tuesday evening and was scheduled to go before Judge Duffey later today. News 12 has just determined that the inmate was Helen Wilkins. The Police Department in

Bridgeport has no comment at this time. We will continue to bring you updates..."

"OH MY GOOODDD!! HARLAND!! I'M SORRY!!" I cried as I dialed his number...

"Harmony..."

"Harland – I'm so sorry – I can come over and..."

"Come over? Why would I want you to come over?"

"Harland – I thought..."

"You thought you should go live on Facebook..."

"Harland – I'm sorry..."

"You thought you should press charges..."

"Harland – please..."

"I begged you not to press charges – I warned you we'd be done..."

"Harland – I..."

"You thought you should press charges – my mother's dead because of you – and so are we – I don't ever want to see you or hear from you ever again..." he said as he hung up...

"HHHAAARRRLLLAAANNNDDD!!" I screamed...

"I can't let this go – I need to talk to him –
I need him to forgive me..." I was frantic. I'd
barely gotten any sleep. I was rushing around
the house, my pressure was high, and I was
shaking... "Le'me smoke this blunt..." I said out
loud as I lit it and pulled on it hard... "Fuck it –
I'll go see my girl – she'll give me a note for my
job – it's not like I don't have anxiety..." I said as
I finished the blunt...

"Where the hell is this uber?" I exclaimed.
I'd only been waiting for a minute or so – but it
felt like an hour... "Bout damn time!" I exclaimed
as I got in...
"Court House Harmony?"
"Yes..."

"Okay – we'll be there in 10 minutes..." he said as he drove off quick. Normally I'd be pissed with reckless driving but I was in a hurry to get to Harland so I didn't complain... "We're here..."

"Thanks – have a good day!" I exclaimed as I jumped out the uber. I started to go up the steps but then I saw Harland going into the hotel... "Harland!" I called out... "Shit – he didn't hear me!" I exclaimed as I hurried across the street and went inside the hotel... "Harland!" I exclaimed as I ran up to him and threw my arms around him...

"Excuse me – I'm..."

"Harland – please – just let me talk to you – I know it's my fault your mother's dead – I'm sorry – I didn't mean it – I never wanted her to die – I just wanted to make her stop – I..."

"Stop talking..." he commanded. I stopped talking and he took my hand... "Have you had breakfast?"

"The only thing I've had is a blunt..." I laughed nervously...

"Come back to my room with me... I'll order room service... and we can talk..."

"Okay..." I sighed...

"You look good in jeans..." I breathed as I pulled him into a kiss...

"Thank you..." he breathed. I wanted him to take me to bed and fuck the shit outta me but instead of taking me to bed, he led me to the table and pulled out the chair for me to sit down, so I sat down. Harland went over to the phone and ordered room service... "Yes – I'd like to order breakfast... I'd like the complete breakfast for two... Yes I'd like coffee... 45 minutes... okay..." he said as he hung up, moved down to the edge of the bed, and looked at me...

"You wanted to talk... let's talk..."

"Harland – I'm sorry... I love you so much..." I said as I started crying...

"I love you too... but we're here to talk about my mother..."

"Harland – I tried – but your mother wouldn't stop coming for me..."

"What exactly did my mother do to you?"

"Harland – you know what your mother did to me – why are you asking me that?"

"Answer me... please..."

"It started with what supposed to be our first date – all those comments about my ordering, my drinking, your drinking – then she calls to ask you are you still there, are you still drinking – then she turns on the gps 'cause you turned off your phone – she comes in my house without being invited talkin' about why the fuck didn't you answer your phone – completely ignores me when I ask her to leave – you invite me over for dinner before you sell the house – I pay her a compliment – I tell her the food is really good – she asks me did you really think we would give you nasty food – then she asks me where I think I'm going when I put the dishes in the sink talkin' about we don't leave dirty dishes in the sink in this house – you show her the condo – she tells you you let this Bitch control you 're so knee-deep in my pussy you lost your got-damned mind – you tell her to apologize she says I call it like I see it – then she apologizes the next day like nothing happened – you invite me over for dinner to your condo – we order from Thelma's – after I order my food she tells me I need to eat more vegetables – I tell you I want to give you a massage – she asks me and just where do you think you're giving him a massage at – like you're still a child in her house – then – when I give you a key to my house she askin' why does he need a key to your house if you're movin' in here – then she finds the key – makes a copy of the key – breaks in my house – goes through my closets – and puts on the strap-on talkin' about I see you like big dicks – I know I shouldn't have put that video on live – but I had to stop her..."

"I know my mother put you through a lot – but my mother's not in Facebook – I'm not in Facebook – what were you thinking?"
"I wanted to embarrass her..."
"Did you take it down?"
"Yea..."
"Good..."

"I deposited the check and put the money on my mortgage..."

"What check?"

"The check you got after you sold your house, paid off your condo, paid off your mother's condo, and paid everybody else..."

"Do you still have a balance on your mortgage?"

"I still owe – but $26,000 put a nice dent on the principle..."

"I'm glad..."

"Harland?"

"Yes?"

"Do you think you can forgive me?" I whispered as I started crying. Harland got up, pulled me up out the chair into his arms, and kissed me gently...

"Don't cry..." he breathed as he kissed me again... "I know it wasn't your fault..." he breathed as he kissed me again... "I forgive you..."

Harland..." I cried as he picked me up in his arms, carried me over to the bed, placed me down gently, opened my legs, and got on top of me... "Harland..." I moaned as he began kissing me on my neck. He felt so good I held him tighter as he lifted my shirt and bra up and began sucking on my breast... "Oh Harland..." I moaned as he began sucking the other one for a few moments and then he took both my breasts in his hands and massaged them as he kissed his way down my stomach... "Harland..." I whispered. He took his hands off my breasts, unbuttoned my jeans, unzipped them, and snatched them off. I kicked off my sneakers and my jeans as he got up on his knees, unbuckled his belt, slid his jeans and boxers off his ass, and put his arms under me to lift me up. He pulled my shirt and bra over my head, eased me back down on the bed, lay down on top of me, and kicked off his jeans and boxers before he entered me... "Oh Harland..." I moaned as he thrust himself in deeper. He covered my mouth with his as he pushed his tongue in my mouth and stroked me slow and deep... and it was driving me crazy... "Mmm... Mmm... Mmm..." I grabbed his ass with my hands and pushed him in deeper as I dug my nails in his ass...

"Mmmph... Mmmph... Mmmph" My orgasm was building like a volcano ready to erupt from within as I moaned in his mouth...

"MMMM! MMMM! MMMM! MMMM! MMMM!"

"MMMPH! MMMPH! MMMPH! MMMPH! MMMPH!" Harland stayed between my legs and we continued kissing until we heard knocking... "Who is it?" he asked...

"Room Service!"

"Oh shit – hold on!" he exclaimed as he jumped up, threw his jeans and shirt on, and answered the door...

"Sorry about that..." he said as he brought the table with breakfast and coffee into the room and closed the door...

"I'll be right back..." I said as I went into the bathroom to wash up. When I came out the bathroom, Harland was sitting at the table smiling at me...

"I'll be right back – have some coffee..." he said as he got up and went in the bathroom to wash up. When he came out the bathroom he sat down and took the covers off the breakfast...

"This looks so good!" I exclaimed...

"They do breakfast right here..." he said as we started eating...

"I love their corned beef hash..."

"I love everything except their yogurt..." he laughed as we finished eating. When we were finished, we both got up and got dressed...

"Come here..." I said as I pulled him close to me... "I wanna take a picture..."

"Are you gonna post it on Facebook?"

"Is that alright?"

"That's fine..." he said as he hugged me and I took the selfie. Harland waited for me to post it and then he took my phone...

"Breakfast with my love..." he read as he smiled...

"You want me to send it to you?"

"No – I'll get it later..."

"Speaking of later – can I see you later?"

"I'll think about it..." he answered...

"What are you doing for the rest of the day?"

"I have some things I need to take care of..."

"Do you need help with the arrangements?"

"No..."

"Okay – I'll give you some time – I love you..." I breathed as I kissed him..."

"I love you too..."

"I'll call you tonight..." I said as I left...

"Hmm – Harland's not answering his phone – okay – I'm going to talk to him in person..." I said out loud as I ordered an uber...

"Harmony – what are you doing here?"

"I told you I was going to call you – you didn't answer your phone..."

"I didn't answer my phone because I don't want to talk to you..."

"Harland – what's going on?"

"Come over here..." he said as he grabbed me by my arm and pulled me away from the door...

"Harland – you're hurting me..."

"I told you don't ever call me again – what part of that don't you understand?!"

"Harland – this morning – you said you forgave me..."

"Harmony – whatever you're smoking – stop – I didn't tell you anything this morning – I didn't see you this morning!"

"Really?!" I snapped as I took my phone out my pocket and showed him my post... "Who's this then?!"

"Hmmm... I see you've met my twin brother, Horace..."

"Hey Harmony..." Yyanna greeted as I burst into tears...

"What the fuck happened?!" Snow exclaimed...

"Is Flick there?"

"Flick – Harmony wants to talk to you – hurry up!"

"What the fuck happened?" Flick exclaimed...

"She's dead!"

"His mother died?" Yyanna asked...

"She committed suicide!" I cried...

"Harmony – that's not your fault..." Snow said...

"She's right – that's not your fault..."

"He told me it was my fault – he said she's dead because of me – he said he never wanted to see me again!" I cried...

"Wait a minute – I saw you posted a picture Breakfast With My Love – when was that?

"That was this morning..."

"I'm confused – why are you crying?" Yyanna asked...

"I went to his job – I saw him going into the hotel – I called him – he didn't answer so I hurried inside – I started apologizing – I told him I didn't mean for his mother to die..."

"Wait – I'm confused as fuck!" Flick exclaimed...

"I know – let me explain..." I said as I lit a blunt and took a pull from it...

"Okay – go 'head..."

"So he says stop talking – I have a room – let's go to my room – we'll get breakfast – we'll talk..."

"Okay..." Snow said...

"We get in the room – he says tell me everything my mother did to you..."

"He already knows what his mother did to you – why is he asking you that?" Yyanna asked...

"I'm getting to that..."

"Please do 'cause I'm ready to smoke with you..." Snow said...

"I told him everything again – I thanked him for giving me the money on my mortgage... then I started crying... I asked him to forgive me... he said he forgives me..."

"Oh that's sweet..." Yyanna said...

"No it's not..."

"Why not? Don't you want him to forgive you?"

"I'm getting to that..."

"Okay – please get to it..." Snow said...

"So we make love, we had breakfast, and I asked him what he was doing for the rest of the day – he said he had a lot to do – I figured he was making arrangements for his mother so I said I'll call you later tonight – I asked him if I could come see him – he says I'll think about it..."

"Think about it?! What the fuck he need to think about?!" Flick snapped...

"So I leave – now I'm calling him – he's not answering his phone – so I go back down to his job – he says what are you doing here..."

"What the fuck?!" Snow asked...

"I'm so confused..." Yyanna said...

"I'm not – he just wanted to fuck you..." Flick said...

"That's what I thought too – so I said I've been calling you – you won't answer your phone – he says that's because I don't wanna talk to you..."

"Like I said – he just wanted to fuck you..." Flick said...

"That's what I thought too – so I said after this morning I thought we were good – he tells me stop smoking whatever I'm smoking because he wasn't with me this morning!"

"How he gonna say he wasn't with you when you took a picture with him?!" Snow asked...

"I asked him that too – I took out my phone – I showed him the picture – he says oh – I see you met my twin brother Horace..."

"Oh my God!" Yyanna exclaimed...

"Oh shit! You fucked his brother?" Snow asked...

"Yea..."

"See – where he work – I wanna see this mutha fucka – he's been lying to you from day one – he never told you he had a twin brother – and his brother's no better – he knew you didn't know who he was – you should file a report and tell them he raped you!" Flick exclaimed...

"He didn't rape me..."

"He played you – he shouldn't get away with that this!" Flick exclaimed...

"He won't..."

"What do yu mean by that?" Yyanna asked...

"I found him in Facebook – I sent him a message – I'm going to meet him back at the hotel tomorrow..."

"What?! Harmony – you can't do that – that's crazy!" Flick snapped...

"I know..." I agreed as I smiled mischievously...

"Oh shit – please don't wind up in jail..." Snow pleaded...

"I won't..."

"I don't think you should go – but since you wanna go – call us and let us know what's up – and if any shit goes down – call the police!" Flick said...

"I will Flick..."

"Thank God you put that money on your mortgage..." Yyanna said...

"I know that's right!" Snow exclaimed...

"Commerce Hill Radozycki Funeral Home – how may I help you?"

"I'd like to make arrangements for my mother..." Harland sighed...

"I'm very sorry for you loss..."

"Thank you..."

"Did your mother have insurance?"

"Yes she did – but I'll be paying for the services..."

"Do you want a funeral?"

"No – I'd like a viewing and then cremation..."

"We can do that – but I need to ask you a few questions..."

"Okay..."

"You said it was your mother – is that correct?"

"Yes..."

"Okay – what was your mother's name?"

"Helen Wilkins..."

"Is that her maiden name?"

"I don't want to use her maiden name..."

"We don't have to use it if you prefer we don't use it..."

"Thank you..."

"Okay – when was your mother's birthday?"

"April 6, 1946..."

"Okay – would you like an obituary?"

"Yes..."

"Where was your mother born?"

"Bridgeport..."

"When did she pass away?"

"Tuesday, February 9th..."

"Who is she survived by?"

"Her husband, June Wilkins and her sons, Harland and Horace Wilkins..."

"Okay – when would you like to have the service?"

"Friday..."

"Today's Wednesday – we can get your mother here and have her embalmed but Friday is pushing it – is Saturday okay?"

"Saturday's fine..."

"How's Saturday afternoon at 1 p.m.?"

"That's fine..."

"Okay – we have three options for you to choose from – the first is traditional – your mother would be placed in a casket, you can have a visitation, a funeral, and the remains are returned to you after cremation..."

"That sounds good..."

"I was thinking that as well, but I want to tell you about our other options..."

"Okay..."

"The second option is a gathering after the cremation – the urn is on display at the service, and..."

"No thank you..."

"Okay – the third option is direct cremation, no viewing, no service..."

"I'll take the first one..."

"Okay Mr. Wilkins – I need you to come in as soon as possible to complete the paperwork, choose your mother's casket, approve her obituary, and pay for the services..."

"I can do that now if you like..."

"I'm here until 6 p.m..."

"I'll be there in 10 minutes..."

"Hello Harmony..."

"Hello Horace..." I said as I sat down...

"I want to apologize to you..."

"Welcome to – oh hello – will your mother-in-law be joining us?" the waitress asked...

"Not today..."

"Okay – margarita, Guinness, and appetizers – right?"

"Right..." I answered...

"You came here with my mother?"

"Yes..."

"I want to apologize to you..."

"You said that already..."

"I'm sorry for deceiving you..."

"Here are your drinks..." the waitress said as she put them on the table...

"Thank you..." Horace said...

"Why did you do that to me?"

"My brother and I don't speak..."

"What's that got to do with me?"

"My father left my mother when we graduated from high school..."

"So?"

"So, my brother resented my father for leaving, and I resented my mother for pushing him away..."

"So you left too?"

"Before my father left, he met with both of us - he left me a condo on Park Avenue with enough money to cover the mortgage and expenses – he told my brother he was turning the house over to him so he'd have to step up and take over the mortgage..."

"That was a fucked up thing to do!"

"Here's your appetizers..." the waitress said as she placed the food on the table...

"Would you like another drink?"

"No thank you..." I answered...

"Okay..." she said as she walked away...

"My brother was working at the courthouse and he had taken the civil service exam so he was able to be appointed permanently...

"How was your brother able to handle the mortgage and other responsibilities?"

"My father left him some money so he had something to start with..."

"That was a lot to put on him..."

'It sure was..."

"You didn't step up and help your brother with your mother?"

"My mother put us both through hell – I couldn't take it anymore – I couldn't keep a girlfriend – I had to get away from her..."

"I love your brother – I tried so hard to deal with her – we didn't even have a real date until after he closed on the house..."

"You never had a real date?"

"Your mother showed up here – twice – and when she showed up at my house the first time..."

"You must really love my brother..." he interrupted...

"I do..." I said as I started crying...

"Uh uh – stop that..." he said as he took his napkin and dabbed my eyes...

"Thank you..."

"You're the only one that stuck around..."

"I am?"

"Oh yea..."

"My friends told me I should've left him and your mother alone..."

"I'm sorry my brother doesn't appreciate you..."

"Thank you..."

"My father left me more money than my brother – he said he knew he didn't have to worry about him..."

"What about you?"

"I was running the streets for a while – I was on heroine – I was in rehab..."

"Your brother didn't have any idea what was going on?"

"He knew – he cut me off – he started lecturing me like he was my father – I left and haven't spoken to him since..."

"Oh wow..."

"When I saw on News 12 my mother died – I was devastated..."

"You found out on News 12?"

"Yes..."

"Your brother hasn't called you?"

"No..."

"Is that why you were asking me all those questions?"

"Yes – I figured as long as you thought I was Harland, you'd talk to me..."

"Were you planning to take advantage of me?"

"I'm sorry about that – I wasn't planning on doing that – but when you started crying and you begged me to forgive you, I wanted to comfort you – you were in so much pain – I wanted to take it away..."

"Did you mean it?"

"Did I mean to make love to you?"

"Did you mean it when you said you forgive me?"

"Harmony..." he said as he took my hand... "I meant every word I said – you were not responsible for my mother's death – my brother never should've treated you that way..."

"Thank you..." I said as I took my hand away from him and stood up...

"Wait – where are you going?"

"Home with you..."

"Are you sure?"

"Yes Horace..." Horace stood up, went to pay the check, took me by the hand, and we headed to his place...

"Hello – I'm Mr. Wilkins..." Harland said as he stepped inside the office...

"Hello Mr. Wilkins – I'm Angela – we spoke on the phone..." she said as she stood up and extended her hand to shake his...

"Nice to meet you – please call me Harland..."

"Okay Harland – I'll show you around, I'll let you pick out the casket you want, and we'll go over the obituary..."

"Okay..." he said as he followed her...

"Horace – this is beautiful!" I exclaimed as I walked inside...

"Thank you..." he said as he smiled at me mischievously...

"Do you mind if I look around?"

"Not at all..." I went from room to room. Horace had a huge 3-bedroom, 2 bath condo. It was bright and the terrace wrapped around to the left so you had views of the long island sound...

"Can I get you something to drink?"

"No thank you..." I said as I walked out onto the terrace...

"It's nice out here..."

"Yea..." I sighed as he put his arm around me and pulled me close to him...

"Sometimes I come out here and sit for hours..."

"I don't blame you..." I sighed. Horace and I stood out on the terrace until the sun started to set... "You ready to go home?" he asked as he took my hand...

"Not yet..." Horace led me inside to the living room and we sat on the couch...

"What are you doing?" he asked as I straddled him...

"What does it look like I'm doing?" I breathed as I kissed him. Horace held me tight as we kissed each other profusely, taking turns sucking each other's tongues and lips...

"Let's go inside..." he breathed. I got up off his lap, stood up, and he led me into the master bedroom. It didn't take long for us to get out of our clothes and into his bed... "Say my name..."

"Horace..." I moaned...

"You want this dick?"

"Yes Horace... Oh God... Yes..."

"Okay Harland – once you approve the obituary, we'll be all set for Saturday..." Angela said as she handed the print to him...

Helen Wilkins
April 6, 1946 to February 9th, 2021
Helen was born and raised in Bridgeport, CT
She is survived by her husband, June Wilkins, and her sons, Harland and Horace Wilkins

"That's fine..."

"Okay Harland – we'll see you Saturday at 1 p.m..."

"Thank you Angela..." Harland said as he left...

"Is that our phone?" I asked...

"Yea..."

"You need to get it?"

"Le'me see who it is..." he said as he rolled over to pick up his phone... "It's Harland..."

"Answer it..."

"Hello?"

"I thought you weren't going to answer..."

"I wasn't..."

"I need to talk to you..."

"So talk..."

"We need to talk in person..."

"When?"

"Now..." Harland said as he hung up...

"Is everything alright?"

"He's on his way here..."

"Oh shit!" I exclaimed as I jumped up out the bed and started getting dressed...

"You don't have to leave – you can stay here in the bedroom..."

"I'm leaving Horace..." I said as I got my things and started to walk out the room but he grabbed me...

"Wait a minute..." he breathed as he kissed me..."

"Horace – I can't be here when he comes – I need to go!"

"So go then!"

"I'm sorry – I..."

"No – I'm sorry..." he breathed as he pulled me into another kiss...

"I need to go now – okay?"

"Okay..." I hurried out of his place to the elevator and took it to the lobby. As soon as I stepped off the elevator I froze. Harland was looking at the names to see which unit his brother lived in so it gave me enough time to duck to the left so he wouldn't see me. I waited for him to get on the elevator and as soon as the doors closed I hurried out the building...

"Who is it?" Horace asked...

"It's Harland..."

"It's open..." Harland opened the door and went inside...

"Can I get you a drink?" Horace asked...

"You got Henny?"

"Oh yea..." Horace answered as he went into the kitchen to make the drinks and Harland followed. Horace made two glasses of Hennessey on ice, handed one to Harland, and they walked out on the terrace...

"Mom's dead..." Harland sighed as he took a sip...

"I know..."

"You know?"

"I saw it on News 12..."

"I'm sorry you had to find out like that..."

"Do you hate me that much?"

"Horace – I don't hate you..."

"Why didn't you call me man?" Horace asked as he broke down crying...

"Horace – I'm sorry..." Harland said as he went over to him and they held each other. Horace dropped the glass and it shattered on the terrace...

"That was my mother..."

"I know Horace..."

"So why didn't you call me?"

"They knocked on my door after 2 a.m. this morning. I had to go identify her. I had to go back to the police station. I barely got any sleep. I'm a wreck..."

"You, you, you! That's your fuckin' problem! That's always been your fuckin' problem! I should've been there with you!"

"You left!"

"So what! Dad left too! Have you called him?"

"No..."

"Do you have his number?"

"No..."

"Do you even want his number?"

"No..."

"Have you made the arrangements?"

"Commerce Hill – Saturday, 1 p.m..."

"See what the fuck I mean? I should've been there – you had no right!"

"I'm here now..."

"You want a cookie?"

"You know what – I'm out..."

"Harland – wait!"

"What?!"

"What you did was fucked up – I have every right to be mad – I don't give a fuck if you don't like it – you need to hear it!"

"You're right..." he sighed as he sat down... "I was distraught. I blamed Harmony but the truth is – it was my fault..."

"How the fuck is it your fault?"

"If I had checked her in the beginning, she might still be alive..."

"And she might not..."

"Why would you say that?"

"Harland – Mom was unstable – it was only a matter of time before she snapped..."

"Don't say that..."

"Harland – I'm not trying to be cruel – I'm just stating the obvious..."

"She wasn't like that..."

"She got arrested for breaking and entering..."

"I know..."

"What if she had a gun?"

"Mom would never do that..."

"I bet you thought Mom would never break into somebody's house either..."

"You're right..."

"How did Mom die?"

"She committed suicide..."

"How?"

"They never went to check on her..."

"See? It's not your fault..."

"It's my fault..."

"No Harland – Mom knew what she was doing..."

"I should've..."

"Harland – you did everything you could..."

"It wasn't enough!" he exclaimed as he broke down and Horace held him... "I'm having Mom cremated..." he sniffed...

"So there's no viewing?"

"There's a viewing, a funeral, and then she'll be cremated..."

"Did you pick out the urn?"

"Not yet..."

"I want the ashes..."

"Okay..." Harland said as he took a copy of the obituary out his pocket and handed it to Horace...

"What's this?"

"It's Mom's obituary..." Horace opened the paper and read it...

"Nice, short, and to the point..." he laughed...

"Not much else to say..."

"Thank you for acknowledging me..."

"You're my brother..." Harland said as they embraced...

"Where are you living now?"

"On Lafayette..."

"You keeping the house?"

"No – I sold it..."

"You put Mom out?"

"I bought Mom a condo in my building..."

"You keepin' it?"

"No..." Harland answered as he got up to leave...

"You leavin'?

"Yea..."

"I'll see you Saturday..."

"See you Saturday..." Harland said as he left...

"Damn – I needed that..." I said out loud as I got out the shower... "AAAGGGHHH! What the fuck are you doing here?!"

"I used my key..."

"I swear to God – I'm changing that lock tomorrow!" I exclaimed as I tried to walk past Harland and he grabbed me...

"Let go of me!"

"No..."

"YOU DON'T GET TO TREAT ME LIKE SHIT AND THEN COME BACK AND ACT LIKE EVERYTHING'S OKAY!!" I screamed as I struggled to get away from him...

"I'm sorry..." he breathed as he kissed me... "I'm sorry..." he breathed as he kissed me again and picked me up in his arms...

"You hurt me..." I cried...

"I know... I'm sorry..." he said as he lay me down on the bed, pushed my legs open, and began licking and sucking...

"Harland... Harland... Harland..." I moaned as I grabbed his head and rode his face. Harland pushed my legs open wider and sucked my clit harder... "Harland... Harland... Harland... don't stop... I'm cummin'..." my legs shook around his head as I came all over his face and Harland continued licking and sucking softly until I rode out my orgasm... "Harland..." I breathed. He stood up, took off his clothes, got on top of me, and thrust himself inside me... "Harland..." I moaned as I pulled him down and fucked him back. He put his arms up under my back and held me tight as he fucked me harder and deeper... "Oh Harland..."

"Harmony... Harmony... Harmony... Fuck!" he moaned...

"HARLAND... I'M CUMMING!"

"I'M CUMMING WITH YOU!"

"HAAAH... HAAAH.. HAAAH..."

"UGGH! UGGH! UGGH!" I burst into tears... "Please... don't cry..." he breathed as he kissed my eyes and my mouth...

"I love you so much..."

"I love you too..."

"I thought I wasn't ever going to see you again..."

'I'm sorry Baby... I'm sorry..."

"We need to talk..."

"We need to fuck..." he breathed as he covered my moth with his, pushed his tongue in my mouth, and thrust himself inside me again...

I woke up to the smell of coffee...

"What the – oh – I forgot..." I laughed to myself as I got up, put on my robe and slippers, and went downstairs...

"Good morning..." he breathed as he pulled me into his arms and kissed me...

"Mmm... good morning..."

"I made coffee..."

"Thank you..." I said as I picked up a cup, and took a sip... "This is good..."

"I remembered how you like it..."

"Harland – we need to talk..."

"Can I make you breakfast first?"

"Sure..."

"Okay – let's see what you have in here – you have Jiffy corn muffin mix – I'll make cornbread – oh wait – I'll make muffins..." he said as he took out the muffin pans and put the over on pre-heat... "Okay – let's see what you have in the refrigerator... you have eggs, turkey bacon, turkey sausage, mozzarella cheese, cheddar cheese, butter... and in the freezer you have... home fried potatoes!" I sat there and drank my coffee as he made breakfast for us. As happy as I was, I was dreading the conversation we needed to have. If he decided to leave – oh well – what's done is done – at least that's what I told myself... "Breakfast is ready..." he said as he put the plates on the table...

"This looks good – thank you..."

"Thank you..." he said as we started eating...

"Harland – we need to talk..."

"My mother's funeral is on Saturday at 1 p.m..."

"Okay..."

"I want you to come..."

"Absolutely not..."

"Harmony – I need you..."

"You blamed me for your mother's death – you said she's dead – and so are we..."

"Baby... I'm sorry..."

"I'm not going – why don't you ask your brother to go? You know who I'm talking about – the identical twin brother you never told me about?"

"I'm sorry – I was going to tell you about my brother..."

"Well I wish you had told me about your brother before I met him at the hotel on Tuesday morning thinking he was you..."

"What did you say?"

"You heard what I said..."

"You met my brother at the hotel? On Tuesday morning?"

"You remember I showed you the picture I posted in Facebook? Breakfast with my love?"

"Oh my God... are you telling me..."

"Yes – I fucked your brother..."

"What?!"

"I saw you – well – I thought it was you – I called out to you – you didn't answer me – I followed you – I told you it was all my fault – I begged you to forgive me – you said let's go to my room – we'll have breakfast and talk – I went to the room with you – you asked me to tell you everything that happened with your mother – I thanked you for giving me the money for my mortgage – I started crying – I asked you to forgive me – you held me – you kissed me – you told me you forgave me – we fucked – and then when I saw you outside the courthouse Tuesday night – well – you know the rest!"

"MUTHA FUCKA!" he growled as he threw his plate against the wall and broke it... "I was at his house last night! I apologized for not telling him about our mother earlier! I thought we were in a better place! The whole time he knew everything because you told him! This is why I don't fuck with him!"

"I was at his house last night too..." I sighed...

"What?! Are you fucking serious?"

"Yea..."

"After I told you who he was – you went to his house – and fucked him?!"

"You didn't want me! You told me you never wanted to hear from me again!"

"So you go fuck my brother?!"

"Yea – I knew who he was – he knew who I was – and he forgave me!"

"You know what – you want my brother – go be with my brother!" he yelled as he got up to leave...

"I want you! You hurt me - you blamed me for your mother's death – you told me you would never forgive me – you never told me you had a twin brother – and you have the nerve to be mad at me?! You know what – fuck you – get the fuck out!" I yelled as I got up and snatched open the refrigerator... "And you can take this fuckin' Guinness with you – I only drank this nasty shit 'cause your ass likes it!" I yelled as he came up behind me and grabbed me into a bear hug... "LET GO OF ME DAMMIT!!" I screamed...

"NO!!" he boomed as he turned me around to face him and kissed me so hard it hurt...

"STOP IT!!" I screamed...

"Is that what you really want?" he yelled as he shook me..."

"No..." I whispered as I started crying...

"I'm sorry..." he said as tears streamed down his face...

"Do you forgive me?"

"Come sit back down with me..." he said as we heard knocking at the door...

"Who is it?"

"It's Judy..." I went and opened the door... "I don't mean to be nosy – but are you okay?"

"Yes – I'm okay..."

"You sure? I heard screaming..."

"We were arguing – I got mad – I threw one of my favorite plates – I broke it..."

"Oh well – as long as you're alright..."

"I am – thank you for being nosy..." I laughed...

"You're welcome – I'll talk to you later..." she said as she left..."

"I'm sorry about that..." Harland said...

"I'm not – I'm glad I have nosy neighbors – we're all nosy – one of us is always checking on the other..." I laughed as I sat back down at the table...

"When I found out my mother committed suicide, I blamed myself..."

"Harland... No..."

"If I had checked her sooner, she might still be alive..."

"Harland – it wasn't your fault..."

"It wasn't your fault either – I never should've taken it out on you – I'm sorry – can you forgive me?"

"Yes... I can forgive you..."

"My mother was left alone in that cell for 7 hours..." he said as he started crying...

"Harland..." I said and I got up and went over to him. He pulled me towards him and broke down...

"They never went to check on her – they didn't realize she was dead until midnight – they came to my house after 2 a.m. – I had to go identify her – when I saw her laying there she looked so peaceful – I was so hurt – I was distraught – I took it out on you – I should have let you comfort me..."

"I'm right here Harland..." I said as I played in his hair...

"Don't ever leave me again..."

"I never left you Harland – you pushed me away..."

"Don't ever listen to me again..." he laughed...

"What about when you tell me you love me?" Harland stood up and pulled me into his arms...

"Listen to me..." he breathed as he kissed me...

"Are you sure?"

"I'm sure..."

"When are you going back to work?"

"I'm taking next week off..."

"I'll take next week off too..."

"You will?"

"Yea..."

"I have a lot to do..."

"I know..."

"I have to put my mother's place on the market..."

"I know..."

"I need to speak to Beverly..."

"You do?"

"The police department was negligent – I'm filing a lawsuit for wrongful death..."

"I'm so sorry"

"I have to get going..."

"I know..."

"I'm not ready for this..."

"I know..."

"Can I see you later?"

"Yea..."

"I love you..."

"I love you too..."

"Come here..." he breathed as he pulled me into his arms and kissed me...

"Hi Ladies!" I exclaimed...

"Aww shit! You all happery – what happened?" Snow asked...

"She got some more dick..." Yyanna answered...

"Y'all sitting down?"

"I'm laying down – what's up?" Yyanna asked...

"Okay – remember I told y'all I fucked his brother?"

"Yea..." they both answered...

"Well"

"Well what dammit?!" Snow exclaimed...

"I fuck him again last night..."

"What?!" they both exclaimed...

"Yea..."

"Umm... why?" Yyanna asked...

"Because I wanted to..."

"Wait, wait, wait – you wanted to?" Snow asked...

"I sure did..."

"Shit – I ain't mad..." Snow said..."

"I ain't either..." Yyanna said...

"So Harland called..."

"Oh shit!" they both exclaimed...

"He said he was on his way..."

"He caught you with his brother?" Yyanna asked...

"Hell no – I left before he got there!"

"Oh thank God!" Snow exclaimed...

"So I came home – I take a shower – I get out the shower – Harland's standing there..."

"Oh shit!" they both exclaimed...

"I started screaming – I told him you don't get to treat me like shit and then come back and act like everything's okay!"

"I know that's the fuck right!" Snow exclaimed...

"What'd he say?" Yyanna asked...

"He said he was sorry... he picked me up... he carried me to bed..."

"Wait, wait, wait – you fucked him after you just got finished fuckin' his brother?"

"I didn't fuck him – he fucked me..."

"I don't know if I could 'a done that..." Yyanna said...

"I didn't think I could either..." I sighed...

"Does he know you fucked his brother?"

"He sure does..."

"What?!" they both exclaimed...

"He spent the night. This morning I told him we needed to talk so he wanted to cook first – I said okay – so he cooked – we started eating – I asked him why he never told me he had a twin brother – he said he was going to tell me – and I said well I wish you had told me about him before I met him at the hotel Tuesday morning and thought he was you!"

"Oh shit!" they both exclaimed...

"He asked me are you telling me – and I cut him off and said yes – I fucked your brother!"

"Oh shit!" they both exclaimed...

"Was he mad?" Yyanna asked...

"He was mad at his brother because he went over there last night and his brother didn't say anything about it – but he got mad at me when I told him I fucked his brother last night too..."

"Wait, wait, wait – you told him you fucked him last night?! Why?!"

"Because I didn't want to lie to him..."

"Harmony – you better than me – I wouldn't 'a told him shit!" Yyanna laughed...

"He had the nerve to yell at me, throw my plate so hard he broke it – talkin' 'bout you want my brother – go be with my brother!"

"See – you shouldn't 'a told him..." Snow said...

"I told him I wanted you but you hurt me – you blamed me for your mother's death – you said she's dead and so are we – and now you have the nerve to be mad at me – fuck you – get the fuck out – and take this nasty Guinness with you!"

"Okay – I take that back – you right..." Snow said...

"Did he leave?" Yyanna asked...

"Girl – he jumped up, pulled me into a bear hug – and I'm screaming let go of me – he turned me around and asked me if that's what I really want... and I said no..."

"I swear – y'all get on my fuckin' nerves!" Yyanna laughed...

"Exactly!" Snow laughed...

"I asked him if he could forgive me..."

"Forgive you for what? Fuckin' his brother?" Snow asked...

"Hell no – I ain't sorry I did that..."

"Really?" Yyanna asked...

"Nope..."

"Okay then..." Snow said...

"I was asking him if he could forgive me for what happened to his mother..." I said as I started crying...

"Dammit – now I gotta get me some tissues..." Yyanna said...

"He said when they told him his mother committed suicide he was hurt and distraught – he felt guilty and he took it out on me – and he asked me to forgive him..."

"Dammit!" Snow said as she teared up and started dabbing her eyes...

"He told me they left his mother in the cell for 7 hours – nobody checked on her – they knocked on his door after 2 in the morning – he had to go to the morgue – he broke down crying – I felt so bad – I just held him and let him cry..."

"Okay – I'ma need you to stop – I'm running outta tissues..." Yyanna said as she took the last tissue out her box and blew her nose...

"I'm glad y'all are back together – he needs you..." Snow said...

"I need him too..."

"Harmony – can I ask you a personal question?" Yyanna asked...

"What's more personal than this?" I laughed...

"Who's better?"

"Horace ain't got shit on his brother!" I exclaimed as we all laughed...

"Hello Ladies,

I'm Harland Wilkins. I know of you by Harmony. I know she's been talking to you and I need your help. I fucked up and I'm trying to make it right. Please accept my friend request and meet me in the room tonight at 9 p.m."

"Did you get a message from somebody named Harland Wilkins?" Snow asked...

"Yea..." Yyanna answered...

"How we know it's him?"

"Girl – I don't know..."

"You think it's his brother playin' games?"

"I looked at his profile – it's new..."

"So what does that mean?"

"He doesn't have any other friends – the only way he'd know about us is if she told him..."

"So you think we should meet him in the room tonight?"

"I think we should..."

"I'ma bring Flick..."

"Hell no!" Flick exclaimed... "Fuck him – he fucked up – let him fix that shit!"

"But Flick..."

"I'm not doing shit – I'm not helping him with shit – she wanna be with him after the shit he pulled – that's on her!"

"Flick... listen..."

"Why you wanna listen to that mutha fucka?"

"Because – he said he fucked up and he's trying to make it right..."

"He said that?"

"Yea!"

"Le'me see this bullshit..." Flick sighed as he snatched the tablet from Snow...

"You didn't have to snatch it!"

"I'm sorry Babe..." he said as he continued reading... "Okay – you wanna accept his friend request – go ahead – I'ma be right here – and I swear to God..."

"I know Flick..." Snow laughed as she accepted Harland's friend request...

Chapter 40

"Hello Ladies..." Harland greeted...

"Hello..." Yyanna said... "I'm Yyanna..."

"I'm Snow... and this is my husband, Flick..."

"Thank you for coming..."

"Okay – I'm just gon' say this – you said you fucked up and you wanted to fix this – why should we help you fix it – we had nothing to do with it!" Flick exclaimed...

"You're right. When Harmony told me that she was talking to her friends, I was okay with that – that's what women do – but when I realized she was talking to you – I had a problem..."

"Fuck you mean you had a problem?" Flick exclaimed...

"I don't have a problem with you Flick – I have a problem with myself..."

"Oh okay – I was about to light your ass up!" Flick laughed...

"My father left my mother when we graduated from high school. He sat us down and told me I had to step up and take over the house. I resented my father for leaving – my brother resented my mother for pushing my father away..."

"I hear what you saying – I get that – but that ain't got shit to do with Harmony..."

"It has everything to do with Harmony..."

"How so?"

"I knew Harmony was the one as soon as I saw her..."

"Awww..." Yyanna and Snow said...

"I talked to my mother about her. I thought my mother was happy for me but now I realize she was threatened by Harmony..."

"Exactly..." Snow agreed...

"So why didn't you check your mother? Why did you allow your mother to treat Harmony like shit?" Flick asked...

"I tried to check my mother – but I also wanted to make my mother feel like she was always going to be in my life. It was hard. I know that's not an excuse but I never learned how to separate me being a man from me being her son..."

"I can understand that..." Yyanna said...

"I understand that too – but it wasn't fair to Harmony..." Snow said...

"I know it wasn't. By the time I was ready to show Harmony that I was ready to make her a priority – shit went left..."

"Okay – I'ma ask you a couple of questions..." Flick said...

"Okay..."

"How did your mother get a key to Harmony's house?"

"When Harmony gave me that key in the box, I felt like I hit the jackpot. I know I should've put the key on my keychain but now that everything's happened – I'm realizing if it wasn't that it would've been something else..."

"You never tried to get your mother any help?"

"I did. My mother was who she was..."

"Why didn't you tell Harmony you had a brother?"

"I was going to tell her. When we talked about moving in together, I was ready to tell her but I wanted to wait until after we went to look at the property she picked out..."

"You should've told her a long time ago!" Flick exclaimed...

"You're right..."

"I hope you don't hold what happened with your brother against her – 'cause it's not her fault..."

"I don't hold any of that against her..."

"So why you blame her for what happened to your mother then?"

"I wanna know that too..." Yyanna said...

"So do I..." Snow said...

"When I saw what my mother did – I wanted to diffuse the situation. I was planning on putting my mother in an assisted living facility where she could be monitored and I was going to have an aide come every day to make sure she took her medication..."

"Medication?! Your mother was on medication?!" Flick asked...

"My mother was manic depressive..."

"Oh shit – did Harmony know this?!"

"Yes..."

"Oh so you told her..."

"Harmony was fed up so she wasn't listening to anything I had to say – she pressed charges – when my mother died, I felt guilty for not doing something sooner – I felt like if she wasn't in jail I could've saved her – so I took it out on Harmony..."

"You know that was fucked up..."

"Yes – I know..."

"So how do you want us to help you?"

"I want to propose to Harmony..."

"Yeeesss!" Yyanna exclaimed...

"Aww... you wanna ask her to marry you?" Snow asked...

"Yes – and here's where you come in..."

"I'm listening..." Flick said...

"I'm going to buy that property she said she wants in South Norwalk. I want to bring her there, tell her I put an offer on it for us, and propose to her right there..."

"Aww..." Yyanna and Snow said...

"So how are we helping you?" Flick asked...

"I want you to be there when I propose..."

"Oh wow!" Yyanna exclaimed...

"Oh my God! I'm so happy for y'all!" Snow exclaimed...

"So you want us to come to Connecticut and you're gonna propose – then what?" Flick asked...

"We go to dinner to celebrate – we all stay at the Marriott..."

"When you wanna do this?"

"Valentine's day..."

"As in Sunday?"

"Yea..."

"You do realize today is Friday – right?"

"Yes..."

"So how are we supposed to get a room, get up there..." Flick started to say..."

"I already got the rooms for you – check in is Sunday the 14th – check out is Monday – the 15th..."

"I'm coming!" Yyanna said...

"We're coming too – right Flick?" Snow asked...

"Yea – we're coming..."

"Thanks – I'll see you guys tomorrow – I gotta get on my shit – I gotta get an offer in on this place – I gotta get a ring – Harmony's gonna be so happy – bye!"

"Hello Harland – How's everything?" Sheddi answered...

"I wish I could tell you everything's fine..."

"What's wrong? Your mother doesn't like it?"

"My mother died on Tuesday..."

"Oh Harland! I'm sorry..."

"Thank you..."

"So are you calling me to put your mother's place back on the market?"

"Yes – but I also need something else..."

"Okay – tell me..."

"I want to propose to Harmony..."

"Oh Harland – congratulations!"

"Thank you..."

"How can I help you with that?"

"She showed me a property in South Norwalk – I want to put in an offer on it – I want to bring Harmony there to see it – and I want to propose to her in the place..."

"Oh that's so romantic! When do you want to do it?"

"I'd like to do it on Valentine's Day..."

"Sunday?"

"Yes..."

"Normally I don't work on Valentine's Day – but I'll do this for you – what time would you like to be there?"

"Can you get us in there at 5 p.m.?"

"I'm pretty sure I can do that..."

"Do you have plans for Valentine's day?"

"Why is that your concern?"

"Because I'm making reservations and I'd like you to join us..."

"Harland that's very sweet – but I don't want to be a third wheel..."

"You won't be a third wheel – you'll be a sixth wheel – I've invited a few of Harmony's friends..."

"Okay – in that case I'd love to..."

"Thank you Sheddi..."

"You're welcome – so – just so I understand – you're putting your mother's condo on the market and you're putting an offer in on the property in South Norwalk..."

"Yes..."

"Okay – send me the information for the property in South Norwalk – I'll send you all the paperwork for you to sign – and I'll see you on Sunday..."

"Thank you Sheddi..." he said as he hung up... "Now it's time to see Horace..." he said as he picked up his keys and went out the door...

"What are you doing here?" Horace asked as he opened the door...

"We need to talk..." Harland answered as he pushed his way in...

"I didn't invite you in!"

"I didn't invite you in either..."

"This is about Harmony..."

"I want you to stay away from her..."

"She came to me because you fucked up..."

"I didn't come here to talk about why she came to you – I'm telling you to stay away from her..."

"How many times do I have to tell you – you're not my father!"

"What the fuck does that have to do with anything?"

"You come here – push your way in – demanding that I stay away from her – she came to me – this is a conversation you need to have with Harmony – not me!"

"I haven't forgotten what you did to me in high school..."

"Oh my God! When are you going to let that shit go?!"

"When it happens to you – when you experience the pain I experienced – then I'll let it go..."

"Look man – I'm sorry Jade had an abortion..."

"No you're not – you're glad she had an abortion – you knew it was a possibility it was your child because you ran the same game on her that you ran on Harmony..."

"She came here last night on her own – she did what she wanted to do – correction – she did who she wanted to do – me – and you can't stand that..."

"When you met her at the hotel – you knew she didn't know who you were – so you ran the same game on Harmony that you ran on Jade..."

"And she fell for it hook, line, and sinker..."

"I was hoping it wouldn't have to come to this..." Harland sighed as he stood up..."

"What – are you going to beat the shit outta me?"

"No..." Harland said as he inched closer and held out his arms... "You're my brother – I love you..."

"I love you too Harland..." Horace said as he stepped closer to Harland. Once they embraced, Harland held Horace for a few moments and as soon as he began to relax, Harland snapped his neck and watched him drop to the floor. After he stood there long enough to make sure Horace wasn't moving, he bent down and checked for a pulse. After he confirmed there was no pulse, he got up, stepped over Horace's body, and left it there as he walked out and closed the door...

"Hello Mr. Wilkins..."
"Hey Charles..." Harland sighed...
"I'm sorry about your mother..."
"Thank you..." Harland said as he started to walk away..."
"Mr. Wilkins – wait..."
"Yes Charles?" Harland asked as he turned around...
"Have you made arrangements for your mother?"
"Why?"
"I don't mean to pry – it's just – never mind..."
"Charles – what is it?"
"I'd like to come to the funeral..."
"Tomorrow – 1 p.m. – Commerce..."
"Thank you – oh – one more thing..."
"Yes Charles..." Harland sighed...
"Please don't get mad..."
"Charles – what is it?"
"Harmony's in your apartment..."
"Harmony's here?"
"I'm sorry – she wanted to surprise you – I hadn't seen her around..."

"Charles – it's fine..."

"You're not mad?"

"I'm not mad – but Charles?"

"Yes Mr. Wilkins?"

"Don't let anybody else in my apartment again – okay?"

"Okay Mr. Wilkins..."

"Harmony?" Harland called out...

"How'd you know I was here?" I asked as I hurried over to him, threw my arms around him, and kissed him...

"Charles told me..."

"I wanted to surprise you..."

"Come sit down..." he said as he led me over to the couch and we sat down...

"Aren't you happy to see me?"

"I need to tell you something..." he said as he took my hands...

"Harland... you're scaring me..."

"You have nothing to be afraid of..."

"Okay..."

"The night my mother broke into your house, I didn't want you to press charges because I was going to have her moved to an assisted living facility..."

"Harland – I..."

"Let me finish..."

"Okay..."

"I was going to have her moved to an assisted living facility and I was going to have an aide come in daily to make sure she took her medication..."

"I'm sorry..." I whispered as I started crying...

"Uh uh – stop that..." he said as he kissed me... "I'm not telling you this to make you feel bad – I'm telling you this because I wanted you to know why I took it out on you..."

"I can't help it..." I sniffed...

"I have something else I need to tell you..." he said as he started tearing up...

"Harland... please don't cry..."

"When we were in high school, I was dating a girl name Jade..."

"Okay..."

"One day Jade saw my brother, thinking he was me..."

"Did she know you had a twin brother?"

"Yes..."

"What happened?"

"My brother pretended to be me and slept with her..."

"Oh my God..."

"She got pregnant..."

"Oh my God..."

"She didn't want to have the baby because she wasn't sure which one of us was the father..."

"So she had an abortion?"

"She had an abortion..."

"Did you forgive her?"

"There was nothing to forgive – my brother played her – but she broke up with me anyway..."

"You really loved her..."

"That broke my heart..."

"I can't believe your brother did that to you..."

"When you told me you met him at the hotel..."

"Harland... I'm sorry..." I said as I pulled him into a hug and he broke down. I held him for about a half hour or so and then he spoke...

"I'm so happy you're here – I'm not ready for tomorrow..."

"We'll get through this together..."

"I love you so much..."

"I love you too..."

"You hungry?"

"Yea..."

"What are you in the mood for?"

"You..."

"I like the sound of that – but what would you like to eat?"

"How 'bout Chinese food?"

"Chinese food it is..." he said as he got up to get the menus...

Chapter 42

I woke up first and looked over to see what time it was. Since it was only 8 a.m., I decided to wake Harland up with my mouth...

"Oooohhh shit...Suck it..." he moaned as he arched his back and pushed himself in my mouth deeper. I lay down on the bed, braced myself on his thighs, and went to work... "Suck it... Yeesss..." I relaxed my jaws and my throat so I could suck him sloppily as the head of his dick hit my tonsils... "Harmony... Fuck... I'm cummin'... I'm cummin'..." I swallowed and continued sucking softly as he grabbed my head and played in my hair. I was surprised when he didn't stop me but when I felt him getting hard again I thought to myself...

"Oh yea..." and decided to turn it up a notch...

"Oh shit... Harmony... Suck it!" he moaned as I grabbed the base of his dick and moved my hand up and down as I applied more pressure to the head of his dick with my mouth... "Harmony... Fuck!" he moaned as he arched his back and shot in my mouth again. I swallowed and continued sucking as I removed my hand from his dick until he stopped me... "Damn..." he breathed...

"You alright?"

"Come here..." he breathed as he sat up and I sat up with him. Harland pulled me into a kiss and pushed his tongue in my mouth. When I tried to pull away from him, he gripped me hard... "Where do you think you're going?"

"Harland – we need to get ready..."

"I'm not ready..."

"C'mon – let's get in the shower · then you can make us breakfast..."

"Can I fuck you in the shower?"

"I don't know – can you?" I laughed as I jumped up off the bed and hurried into the bathroom with Harland right behind me...

"Well I guess I got my answer..." I breathed as he kissed me...

"I guess you did..."

"Let's get dressed...

"Okay..." I knew Harland wasn't ready but I was determined to be there for him... "What do you want for breakfast?"

"I want a big breakfast..."

"How big?"

"Big enough where my stomach isn't doing flip flops..."

"Flip flops?"

"Yea – when I'm stressed or nervous my stomach starts talking..." I laughed...

"Are you serious?" he laughed...

"Listen..." Harland put his head on my stomach and listened...

"What's that? You're hungry? You want some more nut?"

"You are stupid!" I laughed as I pushed him off me...

"I'll make us an omelet, biscuits, and bacon..."

"And coffee..."

"And coffee..." he repeated...

"You ready?" I asked, knowing the answer...

"I need to ask you something..."

"Okay..."

"My brother asked me could he keep my mother's ashes..."

"What did you say?"

"I said yes... but..."

"You changed your mind?"

"Yea..."

"What are you asking me?"

"Do you mind if I keep my mother's ashes?"

"You can keep them if you want..."

"That doesn't answer my question..."

"Let's go..." I sighed...

When we got to the funeral home I was surprised to see so many cars...

"Is here another funeral today?" I asked...

"I don't think so..." Harland answered as he took my hand and we went up the steps. When we got inside we were both surprised by the amount of people inside...

"Harland – who are all these people?" I asked...

"They're from the courthouse..." Harland answered as he smiled...

"Thank you Lord..." I said under my breath. As we walked up to the front of the room to sit, we saw Sergeant Corbett, Sergeant Hurley, Sheddi, Charles, and Beverly... "Harland – who is that man crying over your mother?" I saw the look on Harland's face change and I knew something was wrong...

"That's my father..." he answered as he quickened his pace and went up to him...

"What the fuck are you doing here?" he mumbled...

"Harland... I'm so sorry..."

"Please Dad – spare me..."

"Son..."

"I haven't been your son since you left us..."

"I deserve that..."

"How did you find out?"

"Your brother called me..."

"Oh how nice..." Harland responded sarcastically...

"Son - please – I..."

"Save it Dad – let's just get through this – now is not the time..."

"Can I talk to you another time? Please?"

"Why? What is there to talk about?"

"Son – I don't want the next time I see you to be at your funeral..."

"Don't worry – you won't be invited..."

"I'm Harmony..." I said as I stuck out my hand..."

"I'm June..."

"It's nice to meet you..."

"I'm sorry I had to meet you here..."

"So am I..." I sighed...

"Harmony – come with me..." Harland said as he took my hand and pulled me away from his father. I knew he was angry and I just hoped he wasn't angry with me...

When the funeral was over we went to Angela's office to finalize Helen's remains...

"Harland – have you decided on an urn?"

"No..."

"May I?" his father said as he came inside... "I'm Helen's husband, June..." he said as he extended his hand...

"I'm Angela – I'm sorry for your loss..." she said as she shook his hand... "Your son hasn't picked out an urn..."

"An urn? So she's going to be cremated?"

"Yes..."

"Harland – I'd like to pick out the urn – if you don't mind..." his father said as we got up and followed Angela. When we got in the room, his father saw the urn he wanted right away...

"I'll take that blue one right there..."

"Dad – why would you pick that one – Mom hated blue!"

"I loved it when your mother wore blue – it brought out the color in her eyes..."

"So you want her ashes?"

"Yes... if that's alright with you..."

"That's fine..." Harland sighed...

"Okay – I'll notify you when her remains are ready to be picked up...." Angela said... "Oh – wait a minute – I just realized I don't have your number..."

"My number is 203-296-2926..."

"Thank you..." Angela said...

"You're welcome..."

"It was nice meeting you Harmony..." June said as he turned to leave...

"Dad?"

"Yes Harland?"

"You have any plans?"

"Not really..."

"Why don't you come hang out with us?"

"I'd like that..." his father answered as he smiled...

"Hey Mr. Wilkins..." Charles greeted...
"Charles – this is my father, June – Dad, this is Charles..."
"It's nice to meet you..." his father said as he shook Charles hand...
"Nice meeting you too..."
"C'mon – I'll show you where Mom lived..." Harland said as we got in the elevator and went upstairs. When we got off the elevator, Harland opened the door and let his father go in first...
"She kept the table..." he whispered as he broke down. Harland went over to his Dad, they held each other, and cried. I went over to sit down on the couch and let them have their moment... "I can't believe she's gone..." his father said...
"I can't either..." Harland agreed...
"How'd she die? Was it a heart attack?"
"Yea..." Harland lied...
"I used to always tell her that fried food was gonna be the death of her..." he said as he broke down again...
"Dad... stop... I can't take it..." Harland said as he started crying again...
"Wait a minute – you said your mother lived here – you sold the house?"
"Yea..."
"What made you do that?"

"It was time..." Harland answered as he looked over at me...

"Where do you live?"

"I live downstairs – where do you live?"

"I live in the same building your brother lives in on Park Avenue..."

"C'mon..." Harland said as he opened the door. I was so happy we were leaving...

"This is nice!" his father exclaimed as he went inside...

"Thanks..."

"You have two bedrooms?"

"I had two bedrooms – after Mom moved upstairs, I turned the second bedroom back into an office for us..."

"Us?"

"Yea – Harmony's moving in with me..."

"I'm glad you're happy son..."

"Me too..."

"Mind if I take a look in your office?"

"I don't mind at all – you thirsty?"

"You got Guinness?"

"You already know!" Harland answered as they both laughed. Harland went to the refrigerator, took out 3 bottles, opened them, handed one to his father, handed one to me, and took a sip of the one he had for himself...

"Harmony – you drink Guinness?"

"Not really – I only drink it 'cause he likes it..."

"What do you normally drink?"

"Margaritas and Sangrias..."

"Let's go out – my treat – I'll make sure you have a margarita or a sangria – we can go to Red Lobster..."

"That sounds great – but I've had a long day..." I said to Harland's surprise...

"Okay then – we'll do it another time..."

"How 'bout tomorrow?" Harland suggested...

"Son – tomorrow's Valentine's Day – I don't want to intrude..."

"You're not intruding – Harmony won't mind – will you Harmony?"

"I guess not..." I laughed...

"You sure you want me to hang out with you on Valentine's Day?"

"Yes Dad – be here tomorrow at 12..."

"You sure?"

"Yes Dad – I'm sure!"

"Okay – I'll see you tomorrow at 12..."

"Oh – Dad?"

"Yes son?"

"When you get here you can park in the back – we'll be taking the train..."

"Okay..." his father said as he started to leave...

"Dad – wait..."

"Yes son?"

"I love you..." Harland said as he hugged his father with tears in his eyes...

"I love you too..."

"See you tomorrow..."

"See you tomorrow..." his father said as he wiped his eyes and went out the door...

"I hope you don't mind – I just wanted to be alone..." I started to say but Harland pulled me into a kiss before I could finish...

"We have unfinished business..." he said as he walked me backwards into the bedroom and pushed me onto the bed on my back...

"Where are we going?" I asked...

"You'll see..." Harland answered...

"I guess I'll see too..." his father laughed as we went into the train station. When we got upstairs, I looked over Harland's shoulder and saw that he bought three tickets for South Norwalk...

"Maybe we're going to the mall..." I thought to myself as we got on the train... "Harland – who are you texting?" He didn't answer me – he just smiled, looked back at his phone, and then put his phone in his pocket...

"Hey – we're on the train now..."

"We just got to the hotel..." Snow messaged back...

"Any problems checking in?"

"No – you put our names on the reservations, so we're good..."

"Is Yyanna there yet?"

"She's here – she's checking in now..."

"Okay – I'll see you at 5..."

"South Norwalk next..." the conductor announced...

"C'mon..." Harland said as he got up and extended his hand to take mine. I took his hand and stood up. When the train stopped, we got off the train, his father followed us, and we started walking. I didn't know where we were going and I didn't care... until I saw the Marriott...

"Ooohhh..." I exclaimed as we went into the hotel...

"Welcome to the Marriott – are you checking in?" the concierge clerk asked?"

"Yes Maam..." Harland answered...

"Name please..."

"Harland Wilkins and June Wilkins..."

"Son – you don't have to..."

"Dad – stop it..."

"Okay..." he said as he put up his hands...

"You're all set – here are your keys – you're both on the 7th floor – check out is at 12 p.m..."

"Can we have late checkout please?" Harland asked...

"Sure – I'll make a note that you've requested the later check out..."

"Thank you..." Harland said as we went towards the elevator...

"What room are you in Son?" June asked...

"We're in room 713..."

"I'm in room 715 – I hope these walls are thick..." he laughed. When we got in our rooms I was in awe...

"Oh my God – this is nice!" I exclaimed...

"Harmony – I need you to stay here – I'm going out with my father for a bit – I'll be back..." Harland said as he hurried towards the door...

"Harland – wait!"

"Harmony – I love you – I gotta go..." he said as he gave me a quick kiss and closed the door...

"Dad! Dad!" Harland exclaimed as he knocked on the door...

"Can't a man take a piss in peace?" he laughed as he opened the door...

"I have an emergency – I need your help!"

"What happened?"

"I don't have time to explain – c'mon!"

"Okay, okay!" his father said as they hurried out...

"It's Valentine's Day..." I sighed... "Harland has a surprise for me..." I sighed as I got on the bed and turned on the television...

"Harland – what's going on?"

"I'll tell you when we get there..." Harland answered as they jumped out the uber and ran into the mall. Harland's father ran behind him, shaking his head...

"Son – wait...I'm outta breath..."

"We're here..." Harland breathed as he stopped in front of Kay Jewelers...

"Welcome to Kay Jewelers – May I help you?" the manager asked...

"Yes – do you still have this ring in stock?" Harland asked as he took his phone out his pocket and showed her the picture...

"We have one ring left – size 7..."

"I'll take it!"

"Come with me..." she said as they went over to the counter...

"Harland – you're proposing!" his father exclaimed...

"Yes Dad..."

"Congratulations..." he said as he held out his arms and they hugged each other...

"Thanks Dad..."

"Your fiancée is going to love this ring..." the manager said as she held it under the light for them...

"That sure is pretty..." his father said...

"It's a Neil Lane Diamond ¾ Quarter Diamond Heart 14k Two-Tone Gold..." the manager said...

"I'll take it..." Harland said...

"And I'll take your number..." his father said...

"I'll get this run up for you..." the manager said to Harland... "And I'll get my card for you..."she said to his father as she smiled...

"Where to now?" his father asked as they got in the uber...

"I'm going to pick up Harmony – and then you'll see..." Harland answered as he got out the uber and ran into the hotel...

"Harland – you're back!" I exclaimed...

"C'mon..."

"Where? Harland – what's going on?"

"Harmony – trust me..."

"Okay!" I squealed as I jumped up out the bed, grabbed my phone and my purse, and hurried out behind Harland. When we got downstairs, I didn't ask any more questions. He opened the door, I got in, and I looked out the window... "Harland!" I squealed when we stopped in front of 33 North Water Street. Harland got out the uber, opened the door for me as his father got out, and we went towards the entrance...

"Hello Sheddi..." he greeted... "This is my father, June – and this is Harmony..."

"Nice meeting you both – now let's go see this beautiful listing!" Sheddi exclaimed as we followed her upstairs. When Sheddi opened the door she turned to me... "You go in first..."

"Surprise!" Yyanna, Snow, and Flick yelled as I burst into tears...

"Oh my God! I don't believe it! You're here! How..."

"Nice to finally meet you in person..." Flick said as he pulled me into a hug...

"Nice meeting you to – Oh my God – I'm so happy you're here!" I cried as I hugged Yyanna and Snow...

"We're happy to be here too..." Snow said...

"Harland – get over here!" Yyanna exclaimed. Harland came over and hugged them both, and then he went to shake Flick's hand...

"We ain't shakin' hands – we brothers!" Flick exclaimed as he pulled Harland into a hug...

"This is my father, June..." Harland said as he introduced him...

"Nice to meet you..." Flick said as he extended his hand...

"Nice meeting you too..."

"This is my wife, Snow..."

"Nice to meet you..." June said as he took Snow's hand and kissed it...

"Aww shit – you all gentlemanly..." she gushed...

"I'm Yyanna..." Yyanna said...

"You have beautiful eyes Yyanna..." June said as he took her hand and kissed it...

"Are you ready to see your new home?" Sheddi asked...

"My new home? Harland..."

"I put in an offer..." he said as he guided me to the middle of the living room... "The offer was accepted..." he said as he got down on bended knee... "Now if you'll accept my proposal and marry me..." he said as he opened the ring box... "We'll be all set..." he said as tears started running down his cheeks...

"Harland..." I cried... "Yes... Yes... I'll marry you!!" Harland put the ring on my finger, got up, picked me up off the floor, kissed me, and spun me around in front of the fire place as everyone clapped...

"Are you ready to see your new home now?" Sheddi asked...

"Yes..." I cried... "I'm ready..."

"C'mon!" Snow exclaimed as she took my hand and pulled me towards the master bedroom as everyone else followed...

"I'm Della Crews, Anchor, News 12 Connecticut. We interrupt our regularly scheduled programming to bring you the following news. We now go live to Gwen Edwards. Go ahead Gwen...

"Earlier today, Horace Wilkins was found dead in his condo located at 2625 Park Avenue in Bridgeport. Police are not releasing the cause of death at this time. We'll continue to bring you updates..."

Harland made reservations at Washington Prime and I couldn't have been happier. After we looked at the menu, the ladies agreed that we should celebrate with Winter Sangrias, the men chose to celebrate with Guinness, and we had some of the best appetizers I've had in a long time. It was easy to see why they were voted #1 Happy Hour in Fairfield County as we dined on American Soul Rolls, Prime Steak Tartare, Deviled Eggs, Firecracker Calamari, Spinach & Artichoke Dip, Carolina Ribs, Meatballs, Thick Slab Bacon, Ahi Tuna Poke, Shrimp A La Linda, Steamed Clams, and Prosciutto & Fig Crostini. We were all so full we didn't order any entrees or desserts – we just got up from the table, stumbled towards the door, and got in ubers. Everybody could see we were drunk, but they smiled at us because they knew we were also happy...

"Come here..." Harland commanded as he pulled me into his arms. I'd never experienced this side of him and it turned me on immensely...

"Yes Daddy?" I breathed as I looked up at him...

"These clothes are in my way..." he said as he began to undress me... "Kick off your shoes..." he commanded. I did as I was told... "Get on the bed on your back..." I went over to the bed, got on my back, and moved up towards the headboard. Harland came up on the bed, pushed my legs open, got between them as he got on his knees, grabbed my waist, and ripped off my thong. I watched him get undressed as he looked down at me and he took his time, torturing me as he did so because he knew I wanted him right then and there...

"Huh... Huh... Huh..." we heard from the other room...
"Whose pussy is this?!"
"Yours tonight Daddy!" she moaned...
"Harland – is that your father?"
"Yea..." he laughed as he lay down on top of me and thrust himself inside me...
"Oh God!" I exclaimed as he got up on his hands and started fucking me hard...

"Fuck me... I'm cumming! I'm cumming! Aaah! Aaah! Aaah! Aaah! Aaaagggghhhh!!"
"Uuugh! Uuugh! Uuugh! Uuugh! Uuuggghhh!!"

"Damn..." I breathed... "Is... that... what... I... have... to... look... forward... too... Huh... Huh..."
"Yeeesss... Fuck! Uugh! Uuugh! Uuugh!"

Final Thoughts

Do I have any regrets? Hell no! I'm sorry Helen is dead – I never wanted her to die – especially by suicide. I know Harland doesn't blame me anymore and I know he forgives me, but it makes me sad when I think about how he can't share his happiness with her. As much as I love him, I'll never be able to fill that void. All I can do is love the hell out of him – literally and figuratively – and I do. As far as his brother – to be honest – I don't regret that either. Say what you want but I did what I wanted to do. I didn't fuck his brother to hurt, spite, get revenge, tit-for-tat, or for whatever else anybody thinks I wanted to do to get back at Harland – I did that for me. The first time he fucked me, he had the upper hand – he knew who I was – I was hurt, I was vulnerable – and he took advantage of that. The second time it was my choice – I had the upper hand – I was in control – it was on my terms – and it felt better than smoking blunts, crying, and feeling sorry for myself. Am I sorry he's dead? Absolutely not. What happens between brothers is between brothers – that ain't got shit to do with me.   At the end of it all, Harland may not be perfect – but he's perfect for me.   Le'me go – he just got out the shower, his dick is hard – and you know the rest!